W9-AGH-440

DEADLY CHOICE

Bill Naylor was caught. All his life he'd been poor. Now his association with outlaw king Barry Christian promised him the fortune he'd longed for. A daring train robbery would make Naylor and all Christian's gang rich. But Naylor had won the friendship of Arizona Jim Silver—the legendary Silvertip— who was Barry Christian's sworn enemy. The outlaw's scheme called for Silvertip's destruction. What could Naylor do? Stand by and watch his hero be killed? Or save Silvertip and lose his last chance for wealth —and his life as well!

*Other Paperback Library Books
By Max Brand*

SILVERTIP'S ROUNDUP
SILVERTIP'S SEARCH
OUTLAW'S CODE
MONTANA RIDES!
MONTANA RIDES AGAIN
OUTLAW VALLEY
SHOWDOWN
THE SONG OF THE WHIP
TENDERFOOT
SMUGGLERS' TRAIL
THE RESCUE OF BROKEN ARROW
THE BORDER BANDIT

MAX BRAND
SILVERTIP'S TRAP

PAPERBACK LIBRARY

New York

PAPERBACK LIBRARY EDITION

First Printing: October, 1970

CONTENTS

CHAPTER I

The Rescue

BILL NAYLOR wanted to make up his mind between two jobs, both of which were open to him. There were always jobs open to Naylor because he had unusual talents. He could use a running iron with wonderful effect. There was hardly a rustler on the entire range more skillful in twisting a bit of heavy wire into shapes required for the altering of staple brands into new ones. He had dealt crooked faro in many places, and he was more than a fair hand at stacking a pack in a poker game. However, there are ups and downs in the gambling profession. The last little brawl had laid him up in hospital for two months. He was still weak in the body, and a little shaky in the nerves. And as for working as a rustler, he felt that a man who has been once cornered by a posse of indignant cattle owners and then turned loose has had warning enough.

So Bill Naylor had come into the country to his home town of Kendal to rest for a few weeks and make up his mind about the next step. Being of a surly and a lonely temper, he went out to watch the moonrise on the Kendal River, not because he appreciated the beauty of the scene, but because it was a good place to find solitude. There he sat on a rock beside the roar of Kendal Falls, smoked and meditated.

If he started to smuggle opium, the wages were high, and there was a fat commission on deliveries. Also, he knew all about how to roast a "pill," and he felt that nothing is much better than a smoke of opium at night

7

if there can be a stiff shot of whisky as an eye-opener in the morning. On the other hand, there was a good deal to be said for work as a moonshiner.

The profits were by no means as high, but the law punished the crime with a prison term proportionately shorter. To one who, like Bill Naylor, had spent half his life in prison already, the last item was a tidy score in the accounting. Besides, he liked the life of a moonshiner, the free days, the brisk companionship. And it is astonishing how much life will flow into the vicinity of a little still back in the mountains.

It was hard—it was very hard for him to make the choice. Some of the days south of the river were very memorable and delightful. Life in Mexico, flavored with *tequila*, was not to be sneered at. And the black, tarry liquid itself, with the little taint of red in it, like a stain of mortal red, had a special beauty in his mind. He felt also, that it was a more dignified calling, that of a smuggler. It was worthy of a man's efforts. If he went up for smuggling opium, it was a thing to get space in the newspapers. It was a thing that would make his old associates, wherever they were, exclaim to one another: "Nerve, that's what Bill Naylor has! They can't keep that man down!"

Thrusting out his square jaw, and scowling till a shadow from his brows covered half of his face, Bill Naylor considered the situation and decided that that was a good simile. He was like a furtive, hunted beast that has been driven into the water, and every time he came up for air the law took a kick at his head.

He looked up, still scowling. Opium was beginning to win out, in his mind. And now he saw four riders come out slowly along the flat arch of the wooden bridge that spanned the river not far above the falls. They looked black and huge, for the moon was behind them. The moon threw on the polished face of the river the skeleton shadow of the bridge and even dimly marked out the images of the four riders.

Those four fellows all had their jobs, of course. They

8

were riding in from some distant ranch to celebrate the end of the month by spending all their wages on bad bar whisky. The ordinary run of block-head was what they were, no doubt.

He made another cigarette, and was about to light it when there was a sudden commotion, a jumbling together of the silhouettes that had been advancing across the bridge, and thereafter the figure of a man flipped over the side of the bridge, dropped down, and smote the water. It leaped in a dim flash at the place where the body disappeared from view.

Bill Naylor stood up and stared.

"That ain't so bad," he said aloud.

He had a feeling that in this world one only needs to keep the eyes open in order to see a great many unexpected things.

The men on the bridge remained for a moment, then they proceeded at a casual gait. Of course, it would be folly for them to try to effect a rescue. That fellow had either been killed in striking the water, or else he would be whirled over the roar and ruin of the big falls. H might, to be sure, strike on one of the rocks that pr jected like so many shark's teeth at the verge of the fa but it was hardly better to be impaled at the brin the falls than to be carried down with the waters.

Now, peering carefully, Naylor saw a shadow swirling with the currents. It verged toward th of the falls. He could distinctly see the gleam face and the sweeping shadow of hair worn almost long enough to be the hair of a woman.

One of these backwoods fellows wearing his hair after a frontier fashion that was out of date. Well, he would soon not care whether his hair was long or short!

The body seemed to dally, as though a rope were pulling it back from death. Then the final surge of the current caught hold of it like a spear and hurled it at the brink of the falls.

"Gone for sure!" said Bill Naylor, grinning a little.

But then he distinctly saw the body strike on one of

9

the rocks. It doubled over on the keen tooth. Head and legs streamed out with the downward current. Well, the river would soon work that obstacle clear and carry it down to be pounded to a pulp among the rocks of the lower canyon.

It was a miracle to Bill Naylor, when, as he lighted and smoked another cigarette, he saw the wounded man stir, raise a hand to the top of the rock, and strive to pull himself up the face of it. He had not sufficient strength.

Bill Naylor, without the least excitement, considered the possibilities of effecting a rescue. He cared not a whit whether the man went over the falls or not, but it was also true that a man saved from the brink of death generally feels gratitude, and often this gratitude can be expressed in terms of hard cash. Bill Naylor looked on the stranger as he might have looked on a big fish in a stream. He decided instantly that to attempt to clamber out over the rocks to the point where the man was clinging would be far too hazardous. So he sat down on his heels and went on smoking.

A good-sized log came spinning down the current, twisting aslant just above the cataract. Now it struck the rocks with a crash that splintered it in several places. The shock of it tossed up a shower of spray on Bill Naylor.

"I sit here and worry about savin' lives like a fool," he said. "I hope he goes—fast!"

He stood up in disgust. The cold of the water bit at his body, which was warm and tender under the shelter of his clothes.

Then he was amazed to see that this man, who already should have been dead, was now at the end of the log, and handing himself along the length of it as far as it went.

This brought him fairly close.

Bill Naylor walked out over the safe rocks near the shore and leaned over. There was a gap of perhaps five feet between the end of the log to which the man clung and the side of the rock where Naylor squatted. That was not much of a span, but the fellow could never make it. Through the narrow chasm the water plunged in a solid crystal, streaked deep down with films of foaming speed. If the stranger tried to cross that chasm, he would be squirted into eternity like a watermelon seed pressed between thumb and forefinger.

The comparison pleased Bill Naylor.

Well, the man would never bridge that narrow gap unaided. Should he make the effort?—Naylor asked himself. There was more than a little peril involved. If he secured a good grip on a projecting pinnacle on his side and extended his hand, it was possible that the rushing force of the water would break his hold.

He put his hand down into the stream. The force of it made his arm tremble, and he stood up again and shook his head.

There was no chance to speak above the thundering of the water. And the stranger, floating there on the verge of death, made no effort to appeal, even with gestures. Naylor, studying the face, saw that it was very handsome, with a capacious, high forehead, a bony, powerful chin, and plenty of refinement in the modeling of all the features.

That was most undoubtedly a fellow of force. He looked like some famous man whose picture had been before the attentive eye of Bill Naylor. But Bill disliked the height of the forehead. His own brow was low and cramped and indented. He felt like snarling when he saw features so godlike.

The man was young, too. He was young, handsome, probably brainy, with the most brilliant future ahead of him. Perhaps he was even a rich man.

"Well," said Naylor to himself, "you can go down for all of me."

He saw the head of the stranger bow a little. He had been trying to pull himself out of the water and get on top of the log: the effort was too great for him. He was smashed up. Perhaps the rock had torn him like the bite

11

of a sea monster. And now his head dropped a little—not in despair, but in sheer weakness.

"A dead game one," said Naylor to himself. "Sure a dead game one."

He admired gameness. It was practically the only virtue that he himself possessed, but he felt that he never could have found himself in the situation of the stranger without making some frantic efforts to persuade the other fellow to a rescue. The stranger had not lifted a hand.

Somehow Bill Naylor found himself lowering his body over the side of the rock. He had a good grip with his left hand on a projecting fragment of the stone—suppose that fragment should break off?—and now he extended his right hand to the other.

A cold, hard grip locked instantly on his wrist, and a shock of terror spurted through the heart and the veins of Naylor. For he realized that he would never be able to break that grip; it was the bulldog clutch of a strong and desperate man, clinging to his last hope of life.

Now for the great effort! He set his teeth and pulled with all his might. The hand of the stranger burned his flesh, ground it against the bones of his wrist.

Bill Naylor felt his clutch on the rock slipping. If the cursed water only pulled with a steady force it would be all right—he could win. But there were tremors and jerks; the devil was tugging him toward the mouth of hell.

Then in an instant the strain ceased. He found the stranger floating beside him near the rock.

12

CHAPTER II

A King of Crime

WHEN Naylor was a little boy, his father had said to him: "No man needs to do anything except what he wants to do."

Bill Naylor had said: "Suppose he's done in and wants to faint. What can he do to stop that?"

"No man needs to do anything except what he wants to do," repeated the elder Naylor, who was a strong-willed man.

Bill Naylor remembered that speech as he worked the injured stranger toward the shore. The fellow ought to have been dead a thousand times over. He ought to be dying now, to judge by the way the blood kept pouring out of his torn body. But he would not even faint. He simply kept his teeth locked. There was no grinning distortion of Spartan effort about that, either. The will that the stranger was using was not in his muscles, but in his brain. So there was not even a wrinkling of his brow as he staggered at the side of Naylor. He kept his face forward. He wasted no breath in speech, and presently Naylor had him stretched on the ground on the pine needles. The black of the shadow was streaked with moonlight to show his calm face.

"I'll fetch you a doctor," said Naylor, "and——"

"Stay here. Do what I say," said the other. "Take this first." He took a wallet out of his pocket and held it forth. "That's only a beginning," he said.

Naylor opened the wallet and saw a sheaf of bills well compacted. They were sodden with water, but he could

13

read the denomination of the topmost, and it was a hundred dollars.

Even if the other bills were much smaller, there was between two and three thousand dollars in that wallet. Naylor closed the wallet, shoved the wetness of it into his pocket, and said nothing. He knew that he had come to a great moment. He knew that it was his good luck that had forced him to attempt that rescue.

He heard the other saying: "You can't bring me a doctor. I'm Barry Christian."

The knees of Naylor sagged a little. A great moment? Yes, it was the greatest of his life. Through his brain a thousand memories whirled, each a distinct face, shooting through his mind like the silhouettes of people in a crowded passenger coach when it goes by at full speed. Barry Christian! How many times had that great foeman of the law won mighty prizes? Who in this world had ever gained even the slightest victory over him with the exception of that superman known as "Jim Silver"? And now all of Barry Christian lay there on the pine needles at the feet of Naylor.

Even so, he did not feel the stronger of the two. The brainy fellows who obeyed the law could be damned, for all of him; but this was a great master, a king of the world of crime, and a sort of awe spread over the disturbed spirit of Bill.

"You tell me; I'm your man," he said.

"That's only the first," said Barry Christian. "They've got a reward on me, and it's a big one. But I think you'll make more out of me by giving me a hand. Make up your mind."

In a sudden heat of enthusiasm, Bill Naylor exclaimed: "I wouldn't turn you in if the reward was a million. I don't kiss the foot of anybody to get blood money. My name's Bill Naylor. Maybe you've heard of me?"

"Of course I have. You've worked in Mexico," said the calm, small voice of Christian.

It was the sweetest tribute that Naylor had ever heard. It was more to him than a Congressional Medal.

14

"Go and spill the beans. Tell me what you want. If you've ever heard anything about me, you know I don't split on a pal."

"I know," said Christian. "Take off your coat and wrap it around me. Twist it hard around me to stop the bleeding as much as you can. Get into town. Buy some needles and some surgical silk. Get a bottle of alcohol for a disinfectant. Get some brandy, too, and something to eat, and bring everything back to me here. Bring a lantern, too."

"That'll take me more'n half an hour," said Naylor, measuring the distance to the town.

"And in the meantime I may be dead. But that's all right," said Christian. "The world is made of chance. Hurry along."

Bill Naylor hurried. He ran himself out of breath, made the purchases, visited his father's house on the verge of the town long enough to borrow a horse, and after saddling it, galloped rapidly back.

When he swung out of the saddle he expected to find the body gone. It was in place.

He expected to find it cold with death. But at once the steady, weak voice said to him:

"Quick work, Naylor. Light that lantern and we'll get to work."

Naylor lighted the lantern. Then he laid bare the side of Christian. There was a great, ragged rent that half sickened him to look at.

"Put my shoulders against the tree," Christian said. "Then dip the needles and the silk in the alcohol."

Naylor gripped Christian under the armpits and heaved on the heavy body until the back of the great outlaw was supported against the tree.

Then he dipped the needles and the silk thread in the bottle of alcohol while Christian held one hand over the lips of his wound. The dark blood kept oozing out rapidly through his fingers. But the man would not even weaken. He would not even sigh. Only now and then came a breath a little longer and deeper than the others,

15

and his nostrils flared out a little. But the man was all steel, cold and perfectly tempered.

Presently he asked for the needles, and threaded the first one.

"I don't know that I'll be able to do a good job," said Naylor, his lips twitching in horror as he saw the rent in the flesh.

"You? I wouldn't ask you to do such dirty work for me," said Christian. "I'll do it myself. I've seen the doctors work."

And he began to work the needle right down into his flesh, turning it inside so that the mouth of the wound yawned open for a moment and the rush of the blood increased. He tied each stitch, driving the needle remorselessly through his own flesh. What was worst to watch was the drawing of the thread through the hole that the needle had made. All that Naylor could do was to cut the thread after the knot had been tied, drawing one section of the wound together.

It seemed to him that the work would never end. A fine sweat came out on the face of Christian and gathered in beads. He asked for brandy and took a long pull at the bottle. The sweat began to run on his face. Naylor took a handkerchief and wiped the sweat away.

"Thanks, partner," said the great Barry Christian.

The soul of Naylor worked in him.

"Don't thank me," he muttered. "I'm not doing a thing."

Every moment counted, when the blood was running out of him like that, but Christian spared the time to look up from his work with a smile. And as he endured the agony and smiled at Naylor, it seemed to Bill that he had never seen a face so noble, so calm, or so great.

Never had such an emotion disturbed the dark soul of Naylor.

The sewing of the wound ended with Christian asking questions about where they could put up. Naylor offered his father's house, but Christian pointed out that even in the best family in the world there was not apt

16

to be enough honesty to conceal the presence of a man wanted by the law as he was.

"If you can trust one man in a million, you're in luck," said Christian. "I've found you, Naylor, and that's luck enough for me. I don't want to take chances."

There were always deserted shacks in the mountains, and Naylor knew of one of these. So Christian directed him to cut down or break down two small saplings and make with them a litter which the horse could drag. In that way Christian could be transported to his new home.

Naylor worked hard and fast. He had dressed Christian's wound with a bandage and wrapped him in two thick blankets brought from his house. Now he was soon able to drag the weight of the wounded man onto the litter—for Christian was now too weak to stir his own weight. He could only endure the pain in silence.

On the litter, Naylor lashed him with a lariat; then he raised the litter and tied it into the stirrups of the saddle. After that he led the horse carefully forward, stopping now and then to go back and look at his man. And on each occasion Christian smiled silently at him.

They reached the shack. And there, on a bed of evergreen boughs and saplings, Naylor stretched out the wounded man.

There was one long sigh from Christian. He said: "Leave me like this. Don't offer me anything. Let me lie here till the morning. I'm going to sleep."

Sleep, with those stitches gripping at the rawness of his flesh?

Well, it was true that he was able to do it. When Naylor twice looked in on Christian, he found him each time calmly slumbering. Once he could see by the moonlight. Once he could tell by the count of the evenly measured breathing.

So Naylor, in the gray of the dawn, made another hurried trip to the town of Kendal to make more purchases. He bought plenty of provisions. To the storekeeper, who was curious, he simply said:

17

"I'm going up and do a little prospecting for myself. There's gold in those mountains."

The storekeeper grinned. But, though he was curious, he was also discreet. He asked no more questions, but went on:

"There's news just come up over the telephone from Crow's Nest. The real Jim Silver's back in town, and he brought the crooked Jim Silver along with him. Seems the fact is that the dumb-bells down there had the real Jim Silver in jail, all right, and the crook who robbed the bank was just a fellow by name of Duff Gregor that happened to look a good bit like Silver."

"Hold on!" said Naylor. "Is that right? I thought that Silver had gone crooked at last. Is that wrong?"

For that was the story—that Jim Silver, the archfoe of Christian, had at last abandoned the ways of the law-abiding to plunder the rich bank of Henry Wilbur, in Crow's Nest. It had been a great comfort to Naylor, who always felt that honesty is merely a matter of policy with most, and that every man has his price.

"He even had Silver's horse, Parade," said Naylor in a complaining voice. "It *must* 'a' been Silver that robbed the bank and got away with the loot."

The other shook his head. "It was Duff Gregor, riding a hoss that looked considerable like Silver's chestnut. But the real Jim Silver, after Taxi got him out of the jail, climbed on the trail, grabbed Duff Gregor, grabbed Barry Christian, who was behind all Gregor's tricks, and got hold of the loot, too. But the biggest news of all is that Barry Christian, rather than go back to the death house, chucked himself off the bridge up the river and went over the falls!"

CHAPTER III

A Job for Naylor

THE cabin stood in a secluded corner between two hills, with a thick stand of trees all around it. There was only one drawback, and that was that Bill Naylor had to travel a distance to get water. On the other hand, the absence of water was what secured them from intrusion. For no man looking for a deserted camp was apt to go to a place where water had to be dug for.

So for five days Naylor patiently nursed Barry Christian through a quick, violent fever, and then saw him start to progress toward good health. Every day that brought him closer to normalcy was a day that brought Bill Naylor closer to a golden reward. He could not say how much there would be in it, but legend said that Barry Christian despised money—used it like water, in fact! And how he would pour it forth on a man who had saved his life and then nursed him back to health! It was a subject of day-dreams which soothed the hours for Bill Naylor.

He had plenty to do, what with changing the bandages, and cooking, and washing, and shaving the sick man, and then making trips to town every day in order to pick up news. And of news that was interesting to Christian, there was a great store.

Above all, he wanted to know the fate of Duff Gregor and of the next moves of Jim Silver.

About Gregor, the fact was that the evidence against him was certain to send him to prison. But the trial would not come for a number of days.

19

"Well," said Naylor, "money will get a slick lawyer, and a slick lawyer will help Gregor, if you *wanta* help him."

Christian looked at him with eyes of mild wonder.

"Why, Bill," he said, "Duff Gregor worked with me. I can't let him down."

"Aw, sure. I know," said Naylor. "A gent sticks by his partners, all right. But what can you do? You can't crack the world open like a nut, can you? You can't crack it open and give the insides of it even to your best friends."

"Is that the way you feel about it?" asked Christian.

"Why," said Naylor, "I'd stick by a partner. But when a gent is working outside the law, he's gotta take what's coming to him, don't he?"

"True," said Christian. "But if Duff Gregor goes to jail, part of my reputation goes to jail with him. There was a time, not so long ago, when I could say that some of my friends had been bumped off. Nobody can help a bullet from hitting its mark now and then. But I could also say that none of my crew was rotting in prison. It's different, now. It's a lot different, since Jim Silver got on the trail!"

He was silent, and the gloom which Naylor rarely saw in his face now clouded it darkly.

"I know," said Naylor. "Silver's a devil. Everybody says that. And he's hounded you for a long time. But you've about used up your bad luck, and the next trick may be yours."

"Aye," said Christian. "There'll be no doubt of that. The next time I get a chance, a bullet goes through the brain of him. I won't wait to do a fancy job. Once, Naylor," he added bitterly, "I had him tied in a chair with a fuse burning and enough dynamite under him to blow up a hundred men. I walked out of a locked house and left him to go smash. And that was the time that Taxi walked in through the locks and turned him loose again. And just the other day, because of the way I played the game, I had Silver locked in a jail for another

20

man's crooked work, and a whole town of armed men hungry to lynch him. And Taxi walked into that jail and took Silver out. But, of course, you know well the story of that.

"I've been like a king, Naylor. I've had men around me, every one of whom was fit to lead a gang. But where are they now? Prison, most of 'em. Some of them haven't been caught, but they're scattered. And those that have wangled their way out of prison are scattered, too. The last thing they want is to work with me again.

"Again if Duff Gregor goes to the pen, then the rest of the crowd will be surer than ever that I'm bad luck for the fellows who are my partners. But if I can get Duff Gregor out of prison now that the eyes of the whole world are on him—if I can get him out safe and sound and put him on his feet as a free man again, every one of the old partners will begin to think of the golden days before the pack was broken up. They'll want to run with the old leader. You understand?"

"Aye," said the other. "You have a long head, Barry." He added: "But you could make plenty of money all by yourself. Why do you want to team up with anybody? You could be rich and safe, all by yourself. It's having partners that gets a fellow into trouble. There's Gregor, now. You got him on your mind. But if you were playing a lone hand, you wouldn't worry about anything except about your own cards."

Christian nodded. "But what's the pleasure, Bill?" he asked. "To drift about by oneself and do a fat job now and then and rake in a load of money? Is that exciting? No, it's only a cheap game."

Naylor blinked as he listened. A great deal of this was far above his head.

Christian explained: "But when I had my organization built up, I could speak a word in Butte City and start a man moving in old Mexico. I had big lawyers on my pay roll. I had safe crackers, second-story workers, and every kind of a handy man you could ask for. They were scattered, but they were always with an ear to the

21

ground, waiting for orders. And around me I had a dozen men always, the pick of the land, every one of them hard as steel and true as steel. Men like you, Bill."

A shudder of joy ran through the body of Bill Naylor He swallowed and said nothing.

"I want to build the great machine again," said Christian. "And I'm going to wangle it. But the first step is about Duff Gregor. I've got to get him free. My reputation isn't worth an egg till Gregor's free again."

"I see," said Naylor vaguely.

"Silver!" exclaimed Christian. "What's the latest news about him? Now that the whole town of Crow's Nest is making a god of him, I suppose he'll settle down there and marry the banker's millions and get fat."

Naylor squinted his eyes and shook his head.

"Men say," he remarked, "that Silver and the girl have been a whole lot together. But now he's disappeared again. All at once he was gone, and didn't leave a thing except a letter behind him. And no forwarding address."

Christian closed his eyes and nodded.

"That clears the field for me a little," he said. "But as long as Silver stays on the trail, I know that his eyes are going to be sharp and his hand quick. And the moment he settles down—yes, for as much as six months—I'll come down on him and find him only half the man that he used to be! But I'm glad to have him out of the way in Crow's Nest."

"Look at him, what kind of a crazy gazoo he is," said Bill Naylor, still shaking his head. "There he goes and has more'n anybody could ask for in his hands. And he don't take it! He won't even take the cash reward that they wanted to give him. He won't even let his partner, Taxi, know where he's gone. He just fades out of the picture, and that's all there is to it. His hands are as empty right now as they were before there was all the trouble. What does he get?"

"He gets reputation," said the other man gloomily. "There's not a boy in the whole West that doesn't dream at night and think that he's Jim Silver, riding Parade.

22

There's not a lad on the whole range that doesn't tell himself he'd be willing to die if he could be Jim Silver for ten days. Think of Crow's Nest, now. The fathers are telling their sons that Jim Silver is the right sort of a man. The women are telling Jim Silver stories to their babes. And Barry Christian is lying here in a ragged little shack in the woods, realizing that he's got to start almost at the beginning."

His voice changed suddenly as he looked toward Bill Naylor.

"No," he said. "I'm not as far back as at the beginning. I have you, Bill."

"Yes," said Naylor with emotion. "You have me, partner."

Christian held out his hand and gripped that of the other man.

"I don't thank you," he said. "The time hasn't come for that. Besides, words don't mean a thing. But I have you, Bill, and the knowledge of that makes me feel strong. I have you, and I have one other thing."

"What's that?" asked Bill Naylor.

"Something I'm going to ask you to get for me. It's only two days' ride away."

"Can you fend for yourself?" asked Naylor.

"I can," said Christian. "I can sit up, and I can move about, slowly. You can cook up some grub before you start, and I'll take care of myself."

"All right," said the other. "Put a name to it, and I'll try my hand."

"I want you to ride south," said Christian, "till you come to the Blue Water Mountains. I want you to ride up the Blue Water River till you get to the town of Blue Water. I want you to go into a certain old house there, and down in the cellar of it you'll find a certain room, and in the room there's a brick floor, and under some of those bricks there's a hole, and in that hole there's a parcel wrapped in canvas and oiled silk. Will you get it for me and bring it here?"

"I'll get it," exclaimed Bill Naylor with a savage

23

earnestness. "I'll get it, Barry, if I have to wade though fire for it! And if it held a diamond that weighed ten pounds, I wouldn't as much as look inside the wrappings. I'll bring it back to you exactly the way it is when I find it!"

He was half blinded by his enthusiasm, and therefore he did not see or attach any significance to the slight smile that stirred the lips of Barry Christian before this speech had ended.

CHAPTER IV

The Old Mill

IT WAS sunset two days later when Bill Naylor had his first look at the town of Blue Water. He did not like it. He came in from the east, and the town was black cardboard against the smoke and fire of the west. It looked a dismal town, the sort of a town a man could expect to die in.

"This is a tough job," Bill Naylor said to himself.

He had been saying that all during the two days of his riding. It was a tough job, and it was over his head. He had told the great man his opinion in direct and stinging language.

"What d'you think I am?" he had said to Barry Christian. "You think I'm a whole fire company and a brigade of U.S. cavalry? I ain't. I'm only human. I can't get away with a big thing like this!"

Barry Christian had simply laid a hand on Bill Naylor's doubled fist and looked straight into his eyes, saying in that deep, rich, hypnotic voice:

"I know what you feel about yourself, Bill. And I

24

know what *I* feel about you. There's difference. You add yourself up and find a minus. I add you up and find that you're an important man. There's only one great thing that you haven't learned. No man in the world can take a big job and do it in a minute; the thing to do is to go on step by step and don't cross the bridges until your feet are wet with the water."

That was what had proved the antidote for the miseries of Bill Naylor's mind during the journey. Now that he was in sight of the goal and repeated the same words to himself, a great part of the comfort had departed from them. He watched the smoke going up from the town into the haze of the sunset as he sat the saddle with his horse panting beneath him, and the cinches creaking.

"I'm just an ordinary mug," he had told Barry Christian. "I can do an ordinary job, but I'm nothing to write home about. I'm no headliner. Get that, because I mean it. I can ride a horse and shoot a gun. I've got a pair of hands, too. But I'm nothing fancy."

Barry Christian had said: "I'd rather have a steady man who'll take a step at a time than any of the fancy boys who are sure of themselves. I'd rather have a fellow who doubts himself before he starts working than a fellow who does his doubting after things begin to go wrong. Bill, you'll get farther forward than you expect to."

It was the exquisite comfort of this flattery that had spurred Bill Naylor all the way to Blue Water. Here he was in the town, and he was surprised that he had come this far. He was quite sure that he would not attempt the job that had been outlined for him, but nevertheless he went on to look at the site.

He went straight through the town and came out well up the river until he found the old mill which had been repaired as a sort of cheap hotel. Only, as Christian had said, the word had gone out that it was not a hotel at all, but a hang-out for crooks of some gang. Nobody knew what they were driving at. It might even be that already they had discovered the mysterious parcel under the floor of the room in the cellar.

Bill Naylor, as he tethered his mustang in a grove nearby, began to shake his head. He was still shaking it as he came out and sat down at the verge of the brush, looking at the irregular outline of the gloomy building and at the way the last of the fire of the sunset was swirling down Blue Water Creek. Lights came on here and there in the small windows of the old mill. For some reason or other, though they were not millers, the occupants of the place still used the old machinery, and now the wheel was clanking with a monotonous and groaning and wooden sound. There is no noise more horrible than the grinding of wood against wood. It put the teeth of Bill Naylor on edge, no matter how little sensitive he might be.

"What does Barry Christian want? The world with a fence around it? He can't get it out of me!" said Bill Naylor.

And then he grew suddenly afraid of what the imp of the perverse in his own soul might force him to do.

"Step after step" is what does the trick, Christian had said, and, step after step, Naylor found himself drawing closer to the mill. When he was near it, through the brush, he sat down on his heels again, for he saw a man strolling aimlessly up and down at the side of the mill, as though he were out to enjoy the air and the last of the sunset. But men who are enjoying the sunset do not, as rule, carry the weight of a double-barreled shotgun tucked under the arm.

Bill Naylor slowly pushed around the mill to the farther side, and again peered out from the edge of the brush, and again he saw a nonchalant figure of a man strolling up and down, up and down, with a double-barreled shotgun under the arm.

Naylor went far back into the brush and found the mustang.

"I'm goin' to get myself right out of this," he told himself aloud. But with his hand on the lead-rope knot

26

he paused again. He found that his fingers were only fumbling blindly at the knot while his mind was struggling with the greater problem of the mill and the mystery that it contained. If there were a sheriff in Blue Water, he ought to be interested, also.

Suppose a man were to take off most of his clothes and slide into the river and float down past the mill— would an entrance be found, or would the swimmer find himself drawn down the mill race into the ponderous sway of the wheel?

"I wouldn't be such a fool as to try the dodge, anyway," said Bill Naylor to himself.

But in spite of these good and intelligent resolutions, he found himself standing finally on the bank of the stream, peering down at the mill. He could not see everything clearly; the bank hid a good deal. But now he was sitting down and pulling off his clothes!

He stripped to a pair of drawers. In the water he would not want the weight of a heavy Colt revolver. Instead, he unfastened his hunting knife from his belt and took the leather sheath between his teeth. Then he waded into the stream. He took a last look around. He saw the stars coming out, and the greatness of the Blue Water Mountains, and the whirling of the river currents.

"I'm the greatest fool in the world!" said Bill Naylor to himself.

Then he dived into the water and swam down the stream. When he came close, he moored himself to the shore under a tangle of shrubbery. The mill was right above him. A yellow streak of lamplight came out of a window and rippled away across the water of the creek. The bumping and groaning of the wheel was not far away, and the voices of two men were talking.

One of them said: "I says to Murphy: 'I don't like the turn of your nose and the color of your eye.' And Murphy, he says to me: 'I'm goin' to fix you so's you'll like 'em better.' And then we went at it, and the first thing I know, a gent standing by trips me up, and I go down flat and knock my wind out, and Murphy, he

27

throws himself at me. He was so happy that he was howling like a dog. Whining and howling like a dog, sort of choked, because his teeth were grinding together. And I managed to turn around and bring up one knee, and the bone of my knee whanged him on the side of the chin, and it opened him up like a knife, and the blood was all over everything. Murphy yells out that I've cut his throat, and it looked like it. And he gets up and tries to run, and I get up, and the boys kick at Murphy and make him turn around and fight. But he was scared when he seen how much blood was running out of him, and he couldn't hardly hold up his hands. I took and beat the devil out of him. I got him against the wall, and the back of his head bumped the wall just when my fist hit his chin, and he went out like a light, and that's how he come to have that big cut on his chin, like you was talking about."

"That's a good way to get a cut on the chin," said the other voice. "I heard tell that he was kicked by a hoss."

The first speaker laughed.

"Well, he was kicked, all right. He was kicked by my knee, and it laid him right open like a knife."

"I'll tell you what I seen Murphy do in Las Gatas," said the other.

"Have you got some pipe tobacco?"

"No."

"Wait till I get my pouch. Blast a pouch, anyway. When I just carried the sack the way I bought it, it was always in my pocket. But when I take and carry a pouch, I ain't never got it with me."

The voice passed away, still speaking.

"Wait a minute," said the other. "I can tell you where Smithers left his tobacco down here in the basement."

That voice, also, diminished, went out.

Bill Naylor pulled himself up through the shrubbery like an eel.

"I'll take a look and know what the thing's like, and then I'll get out of here," he said to himself. Four men

28

right out on guard. Six men, I'll tell Barry Christian. It's a job that even he wouldn't like to tackle."

He found himself looking onto a sort of basement veranda that ran under the higher, main veranda overhead. The wet paddles of the mill wheel were rising, half revealed, a little to the right, each one coming up with a shudder of effort, like a living thing—shuddering, gleaming in the pallor of the lamp light, and almost stopping at the height of the rise, and then lurching foward again with renewed strength. Whatever work that wheel was doing, the utmost of its strength was being used.

"Whatever they're doing, they ain't making flour," said Bill Naylor.

Across the veranda he saw an open window and a closed door. The two men who had been talking had probably gone in through the door.

"Some fools," said Bill Naylor, "would try to get in through that window!"

And then, as if in a story, he actually found himself quaking and shuddering, but peering through the window into a cluttered room that seemed to be filled with nothing but rags and scraps of old paper.

He set his teeth. An electric chill which, he told himself, was like the chill of death, ran over him. A moment later he had ducked through the window and was stealing foward, cursing the rustling of the paper. A lantern, with the wick turned low, hung from the wall. He crossed the room, tried the opposite door, and found that it was not locked.

He peeked through. There was nothing but darkness. It closed over him. It shut like water over his lips, and he could not breathe.

"I'm a fool," Bill Naylor told himself. "What do I think I'm doing?"

No voice of the spirit answered him.

Of course, the thing for him to do was to get back quickly. Get back while the way was open.

He started to open the door through which he had

29

just passed, and inside of it he saw two men striding through the waste paper. He pressed the door soundlessly shut and leaned against the wall, his heart going fast.

Suppose they found him, naked, dripping, what would he say? That he was searching for a parcel!

Well, they'd give him a parcel. They'd give him a parcel of buckshot that would blow his head off, and the fish in Blue Water Creek could dine on what was left of him.

"Fish food," said Bill Naylor. "That's what I am. Fish food. I'm such a fool that even the fish would laugh at me. That's what I am. I'm a simple fool, is all I am."

He fumbled foward along the wall and opened another door. He got it ajar half an inch, and, peering through, he saw a little printing press at work, with a bearded, spectacled, clerical-looking gentleman leaning over one of its products, peering at it through a magnifying glass that was held close to his eye. Other products of the press were scattered on the floor, trampled brutally under foot, and yet all of them looked astonishingly like coin of the United States—neat little ten-dollar bills.

That door slid out of the fingers of Bill Naylor and closed with a slight jarring sound. He knew where he was now. And he knew what sort of people make counterfeit money. Any one who has anything to do with the making or the pushing of the "queer" is apt to be a hardy soul.

Well, if they found him in the place, they would simply finish him, that was all.

He fumbled along the wall until his hip struck another doorknob. Carefully turning it, he opened upon another deep well of blackness. It seemed to him that it was deep, that a musty smell was rising to him from a great pit, and he put foward his bare foot with caution. The sole of his foot rubbed on the rough surface of bricks. He made another step, and another.

There was no pit. That had been all something of the mind, a mere fiction.

But there was something important, something significant about the bricks. Then he remembered. The floor of the cellar room about which Barry Christian had spoken was paved with bricks, not floored with wood or left as dank earth. He was in the very room, therefore, in which the parcel was hidden.

Or were there two rooms paved with bricks?

"Sure there are!" said Bill Naylor to his soul. "There's a thousand rooms paved with bricks in this place. And I could fumble a thousand years in the dark and not find anything."

He wanted a smoke with a tremendous yearning. He felt that he could steady all his nerves and make his brain work if he could only smoke.

He moistened his dry lips, found the wall, and began to feel his way along it. He encountered another door. Then he found a niche set back from the rest of the floor.

That was the room! There was just such a corner niche in the room which Christian had described to him.

He got down on his knees and began to try every brick. He tried a thousand bricks, and he could not budge one of them. He needed tools, he felt—tools and lantern light.

Then he used both hands and worked patiently, with strength, on every brick. The skin was rubbing off the tips of his fingers on the roughness of the bricks and the mortar, and then—a brick rocked a trifle under the pressure he gave it. A moment later it was up!

Another and another gave way. He thrust his hand down into the cavity, and his hand touched the snaky, slippery smoothness of oiled silk. The hole was not big enough. He had to widen it still more before he stood up, trembling, with the prize in his hands.

His brain was whirling so that he could not at once determine on a way to get out of the place. But at length he remembered his original course.

31

He got through the door into the darkened room. Again, through a splinter of light, he recognized the apartment in which the press was kept; he could hear the muffled clanking of the machinery.

They had nerve, fellows like these—right on the edge of a town to run a press like this and use the water power to operate it! They had brains and they had luck, or they would soon be closed down.

He opened the door on the room whose floor was littered with waste paper. No man was in it. He went stealthily across the floor. There was the open window beyond which ran the veranda, and beyond the veranda was the black of the swirling river.

He was nearly at the window when suddenly, without the sound of a door being opened, a voice behind him said:

"Goin' to take a swim, Pete?"

"Uh-huh," said Bill Naylor, and walked straight past the window to the door. He opened it as the man behind him said:

"Watch out for the snags. I wouldn't swim this time of day, no matter what the chief says."

Bill Naylor said nothing. He stepped out there into the darkness with one strong, yellow ray of lamplight from an upper window streaming down and rippling in pale gold across the face of the stream.

The two who had been talking on the veranda were no longer there. Naylor slipped through the brush. He walked up the edge of the stream, crouching low, as if there were a strong sun to light him, and eyes spying on his every movement.

He reached the horse. Still he could not believe that he had accomplished the thing.

He donned his clothes and lighted a match to examine the contents of the parcel. Then he remembered his promise, that he would not look inside. He remembered, too, that priceless advice—to make a step at a time.

Well, there was something in that. There was something in that worth more than gold and diamonds. The full beauty of the saying still was dawning on the soul of Bill Naylor. A step at a time, and he could climb all the mountains in the world.

He wrapped up the parcel again, dropped it into a saddlebag, and mounted.

CHAPTER V

Crow's Nest

WHEN he got back to the shack in the woods, two days later, in the afternoon, he found Barry Christian walking up and down in front of the lean-to, smoking a cigarette. Christian's greeting was a marvel of nonchalance.

"Good time, brother?" was all he asked.

"It was all right," said Bill Naylor, rejoicing in equal calm. "Those bozos are printing some queer up there. There's about a million of 'em littered all around."

"Are there?" asked Christian indifferently.

"And here's that parcel," said Naylor.

Well, the nerves of Barry Christian were of the best steel, but the shock of pleasant suprise was too great for him to keep all emotion concealed. He could not help that flash of the eyes and that upward jerk of the head.

He took the parcel and unwrapped it right under the eyes of Bill Naylor. It contained only three small packages. One was of unset jewels. The other two were well-compacted sheafs of greenbacks.

Christian divided that loot into two heaps of equal

33

size. Then he pushed them out on the top of a fallen log that lay across the door of the shack.

"Take either half you want, Bill," said he.

Naylor walked up to the treasure and stared down at it. Then he looked at Christian.

Bill Naylor felt that he was going to be a fool again. He could tell by the tremor of nerves up his spine. And suddenly the words came flooding out of his throat, past the unwilling tightness of his jaws.

"You grabbed this honey, and you cached it," he said. "I just went and collected it for you; that's all."

Barry Christian stared at him with troubled eyes.

"It's all right," said Bill Naylor. "You take that and put it in your kick. I've had plenty of cash out of you already. Take that and forget about my little job."

"No," said Christian in a queer, small voice. "I won't forget."

He wrapped up the money slowly, his eyes fixed on the distance. There was something in all this which baffled the great Barry Christian. It might mean money in his pocket, but there was something about it that he did not like.

Naylor wondered what it could be. There was something about what he himself had done—he, Bill Naylor—that Christian did not like. And that was strange! What had he done except do the most dangerous job he had ever tackled in his life? He had done that job, and he had got away with it. What more did Christian want?

This problem disturbed the mind of Bill Naylor. He was shaken literally to his soul with wonder.

He went off to cut some wood for the cooking of supper, and all the while that he was cutting the wood he was saying to himself: "What's wrong?"

But he solved the puzzle by merely deciding that he was just a "dumb mug," and that the case was over his head.

After supper they sat about in the gloaming, and he told Barry Christian everything. You could talk to a fellow like Christian. You could even say how afraid

34

you were. With a fellow like Christian it was always better to be out in the open and not try to put anything over. So Bill Naylor didn't try to put anything over or play the hero. He told the truth.

He found that it was pleasant to tell the truth. He had never talked so much truth before, in such a short space, in all the days of his life. When you tell the truth, you don't have to work the old brain. You just sit still and see things again the way they were. You see them clearly, and the re-seeing is a good deal of fun. He even told how he had repeated all the way: "A step at a time."

"How old are you, Bill?" asked Christian.

"I'm old enough to know better."

"No, I'm serious. How old are you?"

"Thirty. Old enough to know a lot better."

"Young enough to learn," said Christian. "Young enough to learn a lot."

"A step at a time?"

"Yes," said Christian. "A step at a time, of course. Until you start jumping instead of stepping."

And yet Christian did not seem altogether pleased. All through the story he was squinting at the narrator as though he were seeing things at a great distance. And Bill Naylor was amazed indeed.

Before they turned in, Christian said: "You know Sheriff Dick Williams?"

"That hombre back there in the Crow's nest?"

"Yes."

"I know him. But what's more, he knows me."

"Well, they have nothing on you just now."

"No. But they can always dig something up. You know what they are like."

"I know. But would you go and talk to him for me?"

"Yeah. And why not?"

"Suppose you drop in and see the sheriff and ask him what he would do if the ghost of Barry Christian dropped in and had a chat with him. And while you're

35

in Crow's Nest, find out how things are going with Duff Gregor, will you?"

"I'll make the trip tomorrow," said Bill Naylor.

He went over the next morning, jogging his horse. He had a strange sense of comfort that ran all through his being. He felt indeed that he could look any man in the world in the eye? Why? Well, because he had fetched that parcel back to Christian without so much as looking at the contents—and because he had refused to take his split of the stolen money. He never had done such a thing before in all his days. He could not recognize himself. It seemed that a ghost wearing his name must have performed these things.

When he got into the Crow's Nest, he saw the sunshine gleaming on the big hotels that faced each other from the divided peaks of the double mountain, and the town lying in the dimness of the hollow between.

He went by the Merchants & Miners Bank, which Henry Wilbur had built into such a great institution. Wilbur had done much for it, and the spectacular robbery which had been performed by Christian and Duff Gregor, parading as Jim Silver, had done still more. The robbery had advertised that bank all over the West, and men knew that Henry Wilbur had been on the point of sacrificing his personal fortune, and even his house and the books in his library for the sake of reimbursing his depositors. Well, such things make a bank strong. A good many people swore that they never would do banking of any kind from this time forward except through honest Henry Wilbur.

Well, there *is* a strength in honesty. It keeps you out of jail, for one thing.

Bill Naylor thought of that as he pulled up his horse in front of the jail. He had dismounted, and was about to tie his horse at a hitch rack when the man he wanted spoke just beside him, saying:

"Hello, Bill Naylor. I thought we'd always have to fetch you here. Didn't know that you'd come of your own accord!"

36

CHAPTER VI

Gathering News

It was Sheriff Dick Williams, looking as he always looked—sawed-off and strong and competent of body and mind. He had long ago come to the gray years when time changes the body of a man very slowly, and his face seems wiser, not older, from year to year.

"Hey," answered Bill Naylor. "What's the main idea? You got nothing on me now, Williams."

"Haven't I?" asked the sheriff, his eye twinkling. "Well, I don't suppose I have for the moment. But I can always trust you to start something new before long. What's it going to be this time, Bill? Old line or new?"

Naylor rubbed his knuckles across his chin and frowned. He was neither complimented nor pleased by this banter. He had a feeling that the sheriff knew only part of him, and that there were other things he might show Dick Williams.

"Well," he said. I wanta talk to you about something."

"Blaze away," said Dick Williams.

"I was just going to ask you: Suppose that the ghost of somebody walked into your house some night, what would you do?"

"Ask him to walk out again," said the sheriff. "Why?"

"Suppose it was the ghost of Barry Christian?"

"Christian!" gasped the sheriff.

He kept staring at Naylor, and his eyes were as round as marbles. All at once he seemed a little boy with the mask of a middle-aged man set over his real features.

"What are you talking about?" demanded the Sheriff. "Barry Christian dropped off Kendal Bridge, and he went down the river—with his hands tied behind his back. And he went over the falls and was smashed to bits."

"All right," said Bill Naylor. "I'm just asking you something. I'm not saying that while he was in the water he managed to get his hands free from the rope that tied his wrists together. I'm not saying that he snagged on a rock and managed to get past the falls. I'm only saying—if the ghost of Barry Christian walked in on you, what would you do? Would you talk?"

The sheriff took a great breath.

"Barry Christian!" he whispered. Then he added: "If Jim Silver hears that that devil has come out of the dead again, he'll lose his mind!"

"Well," said Naylor, "I asked you a question. What about it?"

"Talk to him? Why should I talk to him?" said the sheriff. "I've got guns, and I've got handcuffs. Why should I talk to him?"

"That's the point," remarked Naylor. "Suppose that Christian was to walk in on you, would you want to talk to him—or something else?"

"Well," said the sheriff after a moment of hesitation, "I don't know. I don't know what I *ought* to do—about a ghost. Listen to me. If Barry Christian should walk into my house some night, I'd talk to him."

"That's all I wanted to know," answered Bill Naylor, and he mounted and rode away.

When he looked back, he saw the sheriff rooted to the same spot, shaking his head in bewilderment.

At the First Chance Saloon, Bill Naylor paused to take refreshment. He stood at the bar, leaned his elbow upon it, and poured down two stiff drinks of whisky. After that he beckoned the bartender toward him. The bartender looked upon him with a judicial eye.

"No credit," he said.

"Don't be a fool," said Naylor, and he pushed a ten-dollar bill over the counter.

The bartender looked at that bill with attention. It was water-stained and pocket-chafed, but it seemed all right.

"Got your girl's picture on it?" Bill Naylor sneered.

"You know," said the bartender, "there's a lot of phony tens wandering around the country just now. A gent has gotta have an eye. But this looks all right to me."

"Thanks," growled Bill Naylor. "What's the news, anyway?"

"About what?"

"Oh, about things. What's the news here in Crow's Nest?"

"I dunno," answered the other. "Things are going along pretty good. Everybody feels pretty fine since Jim Silver saved the bank. Then he went and faded out. You know that?"

"I heard something about it. Why'd he do that? Somebody told me he was as good as married to Wilbur's daughter."

"Maybe he was. They was around a lot together," said the bartender. "But you know how it is. It hurts Jim Silver to stay long in one spot. There's a sort of a curse on him. He's gotta keep moving. So one day he's here, and the next day he's gone, and who knows where?"

"How's the girl feel about it?" asked Naylor.

"I never asked her!" said the bartender shortly.

Naylor understood. Since the recent great events, every one in Crow's Nest took a sort of family interest in Henry Wilbur and his daughter; just as Crow's Nest now felt that it had a sort of proprietarial claim to Jim Silver.

"Well, I been and seen her once," said Bill Naylor. "She's got the kind of gray eyes that turn blue when a girl gets worked up. She's got the nerve all right."

39

The bartender smiled faintly, as one who deprecates praise of a relative.

"I seen her cut into the crowd when they was after Jim Silver," he said. "I seen her go sashaying right through the middle of 'em with gents trying to paw her off her horse. She saved Jim Silver that day. And now —well, nobody's seen her since Silver left the town. But what're you going to do?"

He was silent, shaking his head.

"There's Gregor in the jail," said Bill Naylor. "They'll chaw him up fine, I guess."

"Yeah. He'll go down the throat. They got everything ready for him. His trial comes in three days. It'll be something like twenty years for Duff Gregor, I guess. That's what everybody says that oughta know. That's what the lawyers say. The town's hired a special fine lawyer to help the district attorney so's they can be sure to sock Gregor for everything that's coming to him."

That was the news that Naylor carried back to Barry Christian. Christian moralized a little on the tidings about Silver and the girl. He said, in his deep, gentle, soothing voice:

"The trouble with Jim Silver is that you never know where to have him. He's not like the rest of us."

"A jump ahead, eh?" suggested Naylor with a grin.

"He's beaten me three times," said Christian calmly. "But the fourth time I think I might win. I think I might take him by surprise, Bill. At any rate, I'm going to try."

"Ain't there room for the two of you?" asked Bill Naylor. "Couldn't you get some place where he wouldn't reach you?"

"Of course," said Christian. "If I ran away, of course, there would be room for both of us."

But by his manner of saying it, Bill Naylor knew very well that nothing in the world was farther from the mind of his companion than the thought of avoiding the conflict. He squinted his eyes as he thought of the thing—two giants, hand to hand. The day would come, and perhaps he, Bill Naylor, would be an eye-witness. For he felt that Barry Christian was going to take him into the presence of great events.

CHAPTER VII

The Sheriff's Temptation

BACK in Crow's Nest, Sheriff Dick Williams paced the veranda of his cottage uneasily. Before him the town was spread out, filling the hollow hand of the night with a glow, and uneven sparklings, and long rows of lights. But this picture, which had so often delighted him, he could not see now.

Every time he walked past the open front door of his house, the stream of the lamplight from the lamp which burned on the hall table struck him and illumined him sharply.

At any other time he would have known better than to expose himself in this manner, for there were plenty of straight shots in the mountains who would have liked nothing better than a chance to send a little chunk of lead through Dick Williams. His course as sheriff had been a little too straight. He had made too many enemies by the steadiness of his honesty.

But this evening there were too many burdens on his mind for him to think of his own danger.

He went back into the house with a quiet step, turned the knob of a door cautiously, and peered inside. There was a screen surrounding the bed. Outside the screen, in the dim field of light from a lamp whose wick was

41

turned very low, sat the sheriff's wife, sewing, bending her head low to see the stitches.

She looked up at her husband with a smile. She had never been more than vaguely pretty. Now the time and work and care had tightened her face here and loosened it there, and printed black-and-purple circles around the eyes. But when the sheriff looked at her he never saw the modern fact of her, but the ancient and pleasant myth which had made him love her in the beginning.

Behind the screen the child stirred and moaned.

The sheriff shrank back a little in the doorway. He could always feel the voice of the child somewhere inside him. It made him sick with fear. It made him want to run away.

He saw his wife get up, put down her sewing, and pass behind the screen. She spoke, so softly that he could not understand the words, though he well knew the voice that uttered them. He could remember a like voice out of his own childhood.

There was a sleepy murmuring, and then Mrs. Williams came out from behind the screen again and smiled once more.

"Do you want to see him?" she asked.

The sheriff blinked.

"No," he said.

"You ought to see him," said his wife. "He's a little better tonight. The doctor says he's a little better. You ought to see him, Dick. You'll feel a lot better if you see him more often."

He drew in a soft breath.

"No," he said, shaking his head. "The morning's my time to see him. I'll see him in the morning. How are you?"

"Me? Oh, I'm all right. I never was better."

"You're all right?"

"Of course I am."

She went back to her sewing and sat with it in her lap, still smiling at him while he stood helplessly in the

42

doorway. But after a time he backed out and closed the door, and went on tiptoe down the hall.

It was no more true that she was "all right" than it was that the boy was "a little better." Women are sure to lie like that—good women are, at least. They keep smiling and let the pain go inward and consume the heart.

The sheriff returned to his veranda and paced slowly up and down it. If he had given up smoking and an occasional drink two years ago, and cut down on everything and saved every penny, by this time they would have enough money to do what the doctor wanted them to do with the boy. Seaside air might be very good for the child. But as matters stood, the seaside was as far outside the range of the pocketbook of the sheriff as the blue and gold of heaven.

"You don't dig much money with a six-shooter," the sheriff thought. It was an old thought of his. He had been a fighting man—on the side of the law—for the half of his life, now. And he never had made money. "You don't dig money with a six-shooter." Nothing could be truer than that.

Just as that thought worked in his mind, things began to happen fast. A low voice called:

"Hello, sheriff."

He stopped walking. He put a hand on a gun before he remembered that any one with a mind to do so might have picked him off twenty times during the last twenty minutes.

He stepped to the edge the veranda.

"Well?" said he.

And the voice said: "Will you come down here from the veranda and talk to me?"

"Who are you?"

"Barry Christian."

The hair stirred on the scalp of the sheriff. He remembered the words that had been spoken to him by Bill Naylor. Then, gathering his strength, he walked

43

down from the veranda and along the narrow path into the garden. A tall figure suddenly appeared beside him.

It was Barry Christian. He knew that somehow with a perfect certainty. It wasn't that he had been told that it was Barry Christian who wanted to talk with him. That didn't matter. What mattered was that an inner sense gave him warning.

He made no move toward a gun now, not only because he was afraid, but because he remembered his promise to talk.

So he stopped short and merely said: "Well, Christian?"

"I thought that I'd like to have a chat with you," said Christian.

"Here I am," said the sheriff.

"Just about things," said Christian. "About the boy, for instance. How's Dick Williams, Jr.?"

"He's all right," answered the sheriff.

"That's not what the doctor says."

"How do you know what the doctor says?"

"Well, a fellow happens to hear things now and then. I've heard that little Dick needs a change of air."

"That's all right, too," said the sheriff.

"Of course it is. All right for you and me. But how about little Dick? How all right is it for him?"

"I'll attend to him," said the sheriff.

"Sure you will. You'll attend to him. You'll attend to his funeral, you mean."

"Damn you!" said the sheriff.

"Anyway," answered Christian, "I've dropped around to have a chat."

"I've had enough of your chatting. Get out of my sight, Christian, and don't come back again."

"Hard lines, Dick Williams. Hard lines," murmured the soft voice of Barry Christian. "I'll tell you what I'll do. I'll step away and leave you to yourself for a few minutes. I'll leave you to look at a little trifle that I brought you. Not for you, but for little Dick. Understand? I'm fond of children, sheriff."

44

He chuckled as he said this. It sounded to the sheriff like the mirth of a fiend.

"Take this," said Christian. "Give it a look, and I'll drop by again in five minutes."

He handed the sheriff a flat, paper-wrapped package; then he stepped into the brush. The sheriff raised the package to hurl after the criminal, but his hand was stopped by another thought.

He went up on the veranda, unwrapped the paper, and found inside what he had guessed at before by the pinch of his thumb and forefinger. It was a good, thick sheaf of money. He counted out five thousand dollars in excellent currency of the country.

He loosed his collar and sat there for a time, breathing hard. Oh, he knew what it meant, well enough. Up yonder in the jail was Duff Gregor, a few steps away from twenty years of darkness. And here in the hand of the sheriff there was five thousand dollars in hard cash. He could send his wife and youngster to a place where the boy would grow well, where they would both regain their strength. He could manage some tale—about borrowing money, or a business deal. There were plenty of stories that he could tell. And when she came back, brown, rosy, stepping lightly, with the boy a bundle of healthy energy—well, what would he care about the source of the money?

As far as Duff Gregor was concerned—well, what was Duff Gregor, other than the most helpless of tools in the hand of Barry Christian? Christian had planned the crime and merely used the face of Gregor to perform it—the mere chance that Gregor so strikingly resembled Jim Silver. If Gregor were turned loose from the jail, what real harm would be done?

So the sheriff argued with himself. Then a soft step approached up the gravel of the path and paused at a sufficient distance to remain covered by the dark of the night.

"Well?" said the gentle voice of Barry Christian.

45

The sheriff started to speak, found himself breathless, and moistened his dry lips.

Then, instead of saying a word, he threw the sheaf of money down on the gravel path and went back inside the house. He sat on the side of his bed, trembling. He was afraid every moment that there would be a tap at the front door, and that Barry Christian would be there again to start bargaining. But there was no tap at the front door.

He went to bed, but he could not sleep for a long time. He could only go half a step into the region of nightmares before he was recalled again to the land of wakefulness and living horrors.

Once, as full consciousness returned to him, he saw a white form seated beside the window, and he knew that it was his wife sitting there, thinking.

He got out of bed and put his hand on her bare shoulder. Her flesh was dank and cold, like the coolness of dead bodies. He told her to get into bed, that she would have to sleep.

She said, without looking up: "I don't want to go to bed. I don't want to admit the day has ended."

Well, he understood that, too. If this day ended, Heaven alone could tell what the next day would bring. The next day might be the last day for which they were waiting. The next day might not dawn at all for little Dick.

"Things are going to be all right," said the sheriff. "You go to bed. I'll go in and sit there with Dickie."

"*You* sit there? Are you out of your head? Have you lost your mind?" she exclaimed. "What are you thinking of? Take care of your crooks and thugs and jailbirds, but let Dickie alone. Unless you want to frighten him into the grave."

She never had talked like this before. She would not be talking like this now, he knew, except that she was strained to the breaking point. He stood back in a corner, silent, until she snapped at him:

46

"Go back to bed! I don't want you here. You're no comfort to him."

He said nothing. Perhaps it was not all nerves, he told himself. Perhaps she meant what she said. Perhaps she never had cared much about him. Women can do that; they can cover up the truth for years and years. In great criminal cases you find women who are capable of acting like that.

So his heart grew old and small in him as he considered the dreadful possibilities of her unknown mind.

"Are you going to bed?" she snapped again.

"When you do," he told her.

She got up. He thought that she was going to throw herself at his throat. Instead, she ran to the bed and flung herself into it, face down. He went to the bed and covered her up. She began to cry softly. Now and then a great sob would break out. She fought with writhings of the body to keep the noise inside her for fear lest it might disturb the boy in the next room.

"Don't let me make a noise! Don't wake him up!" she said.

The sheriff put his hand on her bare, cold shoulder, and sat silently in the darkness.

After a time the sobbing ceased. She lay panting, and out of her panting she said finally:

"Oh, Dick, my heart's broken! Nothing can save him. He's worse every day."

"Listen!" said the sheriff.

"Yes?" she said.

"Listen to me. I'm going to do something," said the sheriff.

She made a moaning sound for an answer. They spoke no more. He pulled a chair up beside the bed and sat in it all night long, without sleeping. He put his hand on the bed. Sometimes she caught at the hand in her sleep and clung to it. At other times she threw it away.

In the morning the sheriff bathed in a tub of cold water, shaved, dressed, and went down to the jail. He

47

walked up and down the cell aisles. There were twenty men in the jail this morning. Half of them were disturbers of the peace; half of them were old offenders. He looked all of those old offenders in the eye and decided that his criticism of them in the past had always been rather too harsh.

He was so full of thoughts on this day that he could hardly give attention to a single item of business.

Late in the afternoon word came in that young Crowley was over in the First Chance Saloon smashing things up, dead drunk, and crazier than ever. The peculiarity of young Crowley was that the more drunk he grew, the straighter he shot.

But the sheriff did not wait to raise a posse. He did not even take a gun. He got up from his office chair and went right over the way he was, bare-headed, and went into the First Chance Saloon, smiling faintly.

Young Crowley stood down at the other end of the bar and fired three bullets. One of them clipped a lock off the head of the sheriff. But that didn't matter. It was simply a relief to have something to do with his hands, the sheriff thought. And he went up to Crowley and put a hand on his shoulder.

"I'm going to break you open," said Crowley.

"Sure you are," agreed the sheriff, "but you're coming along with me first, so that we can have a quiet little talk together."

"If anybody tries to keep us from having a talk," said Crowley, "I'll salt 'em down with lead."

So the sheriff walked him harmlessly back to the jail and took the weapons away from him and locked him up. Afterward, as Crowley lay face downward on the cot in his cell, snoring loudly, the sheriff stood by and looked at him with an almost envious eye.

Crowley had simply been breaking the peace in a rather obnoxious manner. That was all that Crowley would have to answer for in the court. There would be nothing important on the mind or the conscience of Crowley. And the sheriff?

Well, Heaven alone could tell what he would have to answer for before another day was chalked up on the calendar.

When he got home that night he could hardly eat his supper, because young Dick was having a choking and coughing fit, and in between the spells the sheriff could hear him panting. Mrs. Williams kept running back and forth between the dining room and the sick boy. But she was very cheerful and affectionate. She kept smiling and shining her eyes at the sheriff. And the sheriff understood. She was making amends for her behavior of the night before.

As if she needed to make amends! As if she could not spend the rest of her life kicking him in the face!

Well, after supper he went out into the darkness of the veranda and sat still, smoking his pipe.

There was plenty of wealth in the world. There was plenty of money right there in Crow's Nest. And he knew how to get it.

If people paid a man the salary of a dog catcher and asked him to take the duties of a sheriff, what could they expect of him?

Then he heard a soft voice say out of the darkness: "Evening, sheriff. May I have a chat with you?"

The sheriff closed his eyes and knew that this was the softness of the voice of the devil, uttering temptation. He stood up, his eyes still half closed, and blundered down the steps and into the garden path.

49

CHAPTER VIII

Gregor's Escape

CHRISTIAN, walking jauntily up and down in front of the little cabin in the woods near the town of Kendal, said: "Now, Bill, it's time that we should begin to do something."

Bill Naylor sat on a stump whittling at a piece of soft white pine which furled away from the edge of his sharp knife in translucent slivers. He squinted at his whittling as though he were trying to make sure that the stick was shaping straight and true; in reality, he was thinking about his ride to Blue Water, and wondering what Barry Christian meant by "doing something" if that trip to Blue Water had not been "something."

Then he regarded the tall body and the long, pale, handsome face of Barry Christian, so full of mobility and expression.

"All right," said Bill Naylor.

A squirrel came out on a branch and chattered down at them, bobbing its tail as rapidly as it barked. Christian with a fluid gesture, produced an oversized Colt from under his coat and shot the squirrel off the branch. It dropped at a distance, a red smudge on the pine needles. Naylor stopped whittling and regarded that little blur against the ground. Even children in that part of the world could take a squirrel out of a tree with a rifle, but revolver work was another matter. The great feats of revolver marksmanship were generally talked about, and rarely seen.

50

Christian said: "Now we can talk in quiet—and in private, eh?"

The remark pleased Naylor very little. The laughter pleased him not at all. There were certain features in the character of the great Barry Christian which were not ideal. That, in short, was the truth, though Bill Naylor still valiantly strove to close his eyes to the unpleasant truth. Of course, the man was a criminal, but he must be a great, important, classic example of crime, not one to do casual murder even on a squirrel.

Bill Naylor forcibly removed his mind from these thoughts.

"All right, chief," said he. "We'll do something, then."

"In the first place," said Christian, "we must pick up Duff Gregor."

"Sure," said Naylor. "All we gotta do is to break the jail, and then, after we've unlocked his cell and taken off his irons, we can pick him up. That oughta be easy!"

His irony had small effect on Barry Christian, who merely said:

"Well, it may not be so complicated. Let me tell you what I'd like to have you do."

"Fire away," said Naylor.

"First I want you to go through town—Kendal, yonder—and buy a good, fast, tough mustang. Then I want you to drift down to Crow's Nest."

"Right."

"You know the southwest corner of the vacant lot the jail stands in, in Crow's Nest?"

"Yes, I know."

"Go there with your two horses after dark, and wait in the grove of saplings. Pretty soon a man will walk into those trees and call out in a quiet voice, 'Barry!' You will answer 'Waiting!' Can you remember that?"

"Yes. Who will the man be?"

"Why, the man will be Duff Gregor."

"The devil he will be!"

"Not the devil. Just Duff Gregor. There's plenty of bluff, but not much devil in Duff Gregor."

"How'll he get out of the jail? Bribery?"

"What a thing to say!" replied Christian. "Bribery? How could that be? No, no. Gregor will break out at a time when the sheriff is in the jail all by himself. At a time when the sheriff, in fact, has made sure that all is well, and has gone into his office to do some paper work. At that time the door of the cell of Gregor will push open, just as though the sheriff had unlocked it. And Gregor will steal out, just as if the sheriff had thrown him the key for his manacles. Gregor will go to the side door, and with another key he'll unlock that. And then he'll step out into the night and walk straight to you. Understand?"

"By thunder," said Naylor, "you even managed to get to Dick Williams? You can do anything, then!"

"Give me a purse of the right size and I'll find any man's price," boasted Christian. "It's simple enough. But you'll be there with two horses waiting, and you and Gregor will ride out of Crow's Nest—keeping to the by lanes—and head straight on down the valley till you come to the river. You'll trail along beside the river till you reach the island. You'll probably be able to wade the horses across to the island. If not, and if the river's high and fast, you can swim them across. When you reach the island, I'll probably be there, waiting for you. If not, take the trail I told you about to that deserted ranch. Better take along some provisions in case we need 'em later."

"I'll do what you say," said Naylor.

"You don't seem happy about it, Bill," suggested Barry Christian. "What's the matter?"

"Me? Aw, I'm happy enough. I'm just wondering where the whole job is heading."

"As long as you work with me, old-timer," said Christian, "you can always be sure that every job is heading for easy money."

"Unless there's a Jim Silver in the way."

From Christian there was a silence after this remark. Bill Naylor, rather frightened by the silence, stood up

52

and prepared to leave at once. He promised himself that he would make no more cracks about the great Jim Silver—not in the presence of Barry Christian.

So, saddling his mustang, Bill Naylor started at once for Kendal town, first rehearsing to Christian exactly what he should do. All of the instructions were firmly in his mind before he left, and he jogged the patient mustang through the sweeping shadows of the pine woods and out into the blue and green and gold of the open day.

In Kendal he got an excellent mustang, mean, but as tough as leather. The meaner the mustang, the more wear to it, is a regular precept in the West.

He made a few purchases of provisions in Kendal, and then resumed the journey in a very leisurely manner. In fact, he had to kill two hours in idleness outside of Crow's Nest before the coming of sunset, when he was free to enter the town.

As he passed down the streets and saw the lamplight streaking out of the houses, he kept saying to himself that behind every house there was the fortune and the strength of a most corruptible man. If Dick Williams had been bought, then any man could be bought, and Barry Christian was right. Every man in the world could be bought, except, let us say, Jim Silver.

And he was a freak. He didn't count!

When Naylor came to the big vacant space in the center of which the jail stood, it was pitch-dark. All the houses were subdued, and only occasional voices came drifting through the open windows from supper tables.

In the dark of the grove of saplings he waited, holding the lead ropes of the two horses. He grew tired of standing, and sat down on his heels, then cross-legged, like an Indian.

He expected to hear an outbreak of shouting from the jail, first of all, since it did not seem possible that even with the sheriff's connivance a criminal could escape without making some disturbance. Instead, it happened

53

exactly as the great Barry Christian had predicted. There was simply the sound of a quiet voice, calling, in a tone that could not be heard more than ten steps away: "Barry! Barry!"

Bill Naylor could have whistled with surprise. It proved to him that Barry Christian, when he laid a plan, knew how to have one part dovetail with another.

Naylor gave the answer, and instantly a dim shadow appeared before him among the trees as he rose to his feet.

"You're from what?" asked the stranger.

"Barry. And you're Duff?"

"Shut up!" gasped the stranger. "Shut up, you fool!"

Naylor grinned into the darkness. After all, Gregor had not been spending time in jail for fun, and it was no wonder that his nerves were a little bit frayed out.

"All right," said Naylor. "Here's your pony. Here, on the near side. Mind—it's likely to pitch. I took out most of the kinks to-day, but there may still be a few left."

Duff Gregor mounted. He was so big that he made the horse look small as a pony indeed. But no wonder he was big. A man who passed for Jim Silver had to have inches, at the least.

Naylor repeated the instructions in a quiet voice.

The only remark of Gregor was: "The island in the lower river is too close to Crow's Nest. A thousand miles is what ought to be between me and this town. They're all going to be out on my trail before half an hour."

Naylor led the way out of the trees. They jogged across the lot, turned down an alley toward the left, and then made the first right turn, and as they entered this new lane, bad luck overtook them.

A house door beside them swung open suddenly, and as a pair of men came out, the shaft of the lamplight struck full on Gregor. The mustang, startled, reared up, and in so doing, held Gregor in the light for an instant and caused the brim of his sombrero to flare away from his face.

As the horse pitched forward again, well-ridden, a voice said from the porch of the house:

"That's Jim Silver, by thunder!"

And the other voice gasped: "No, that's Duff Gregor —out of jail!"

CHAPTER IX

The Pursuit

BILL NAYLOR felt that it might be only a guess that would be lost in the darkness of the night; he kept his horse to a dog-trot and muttered to big Duff Gregor to do the same, but a moment later a gun exploded three times, and two wild voices yelled in chorus:

"Turn out! Turn out! Gregor's on the loose! Duff Gregor's on his way!"

Could the devil himself have planned the thing more perfectly? Could that door have been opened more inopportunely?

There was nothing for it but to spur the horses. They went through the rest of Crow's Nest at a dead run, and behind them, whirling up into the sky, floating dimly in their ears, was the racket of the gathering pursuit.

For the people of Crow's Nest were not such city dwellers that they had become pedestrians. In front of nearly every house there was sure to be at least one horse tethered. And every man, almost, carried a gun. In ten seconds a man seated quietly at his supper table could be under way, riding like mad in a chase. It was like tapping a wasp's nest and then trying to get away, with the wasps in hot pursuit of the first moving object.

The uproar spread as fast as they could ride; and as

they shot out of town and took the dangerous, long down grade toward the bottom of the valley beyond, a man who had run out of his house at the sound of the shouting dropped to one knee and opened on the two fugitives with a rifle. They whirled by some trees, and heard the bullets fly among the branches.

Luckily they had two good horses which could run and stand the gaff for a long time. How good they would prove matched against the very best that the young bloods of Crow's Nest could bring into the field remained to be seen. The bulk of Duff Gregor made Bill Naylor shake his head.

They got down the slope with the pursuit thundering halfway down the hill behind them. Now they had either a straight road to follow, or else there were the open fields toward the river. The road was too dangerous, for at any time they might run into a party of riders from the opposite direction and be hailed to stop. So they took to the fields at the shouted advice of Naylor.

The turf was good; the ground was firm; the horses flew along with doubled speed. The cool, sweet smell of the grass came off the ground. The night had no moon. Before them they could see patches of trees here and there, and willows receded far from the bank of the river now and again, marking out marshy places. If it came to a pinch, they might be able to hide in one of those patches and try to swim the river.

The river, however, was by no means a promising sight. Usually it kept well behind its banks, but there must have been a freshet somewhere among its tributaries in the higher mountains, for now the starlight glistened on wide, still flats of standing water, where the stream had overflowed. Twice their horses spattered through the edges of these floods, and half bogged down in the steep going.

Behind them came the men of Crow's Nest. Bill Naylor saw them spread out like a great fan, which kept growing longer and longer in the handle as the slower

56

riders fell back and the faster ones with a later start speeded up from behind.

Naylor shook his head. By the way the head of that fan was creeping up on them, he could tell what sort of horses and riders there were in the outfit. He could almost see the beauty of the horses and the keen riders leaning forward to jockey the utmost speed out of the mounts.

If Barry Christian had been there—well, what could even a Barry Christian think of a time like that? The paralyzing fear of flight began to thicken the blood of Bill Naylor. Once he jerked out a revolver and turned with a beastly, snarling desire to fire blindly back at the pursers.

Something stopped his hand. Besides, if it came to shooting the thing out at close range, he would want well-filled chambers in his guns.

Then the horse of Duff Gregor stumbled, groaned like a stricken man, and went on, limping heavily.

"What sort of a cheap plug did you bring me?" yelled Gregor. "They're goin' to get me They're goin' to swallow me up again. You bring me a cheap, second-hand plug like this and expect me to do anything with it?"

Naylor said nothing. His whirling mind could not evolve any words, but gallantly he pulled down the gait of his own horse to the labored strivings of Gregor's mustang. Behind them the men of Crow's Nest ever were looming larger and larger.

If only the Indian yelling would stop! But it increased each instant, rising in a wild chorus of joy. Guns exploded rapidly. They were not aimed at the fleeing pair; they were fired in mere excess of happiness as the riders found the quarry coming into their hand.

Then Naylor knew the one thing that remained for them to try. He waved toward the river and yelled:

"Take to the water!"

"I'd rather hang than drown!" shouted Duff Gregor.

Well, it looked like that, right enough. Even the starlight was enough to show the dangerous face of the

57

river, the irregular swirling of the currents, and here and there a rifle lifting from the surface like the fin of a great fish.

But it was the only thing.

Once, with a crew of other youngsters, Bill Naylor ran down a wounded deer until it took to the rapid of a river that was more white water than blue. He remembered how the beautiful animal remained for an instant on the bank, pointing its nose at the sky and trailing the sweep of its horns over its back. Then, despairingly, it leaped. It swam well. Bill Naylor, from the bank, secretly hoped that it would safely make the ford. But his companions, savagely yelling, opened fire on the small, struggling head and shoulders.

No bullets hit. No bullets were needed. In the center of the stream the current suddenly mastered the poor fugitive and sent it whirling down to the cascade.

Well, this was very much like that. There was no real safety in the water, but treacherous currents were better than the rifles and the jails of savage men.

So Naylor swung straight in toward the bank, crying: "This way or no way. Don't be a fool, Gregor!"

A stream of howling curses answered him, but Gregor obediently followed, driving his lamed horse right at the bank.

It was not two feet above the top of the flood. The good mustang that carried Naylor knew water as well as land, and dipped one step down the bank, then lunged far out into the current. Slipping out of the saddle, he took the horse by the tail and swam with kicking feet and with the strokes of his other hand.

He looked back. Already an immensity of water seemed to stretch between him and the shore. That water had the sheen of polished metal. But metal cannot give back such shifting and changing lights.

He saw the lame horse of Duff Gregor swimming only a little to his rear. He could make out the head quite clearly, and the flaring of the nostrils and the pricking of the gallant ears. Lame or not, it seemed able to swim

58

as well as Naylor's horse. Behind it there was a good deal of threshing and foaming as Duff Gregor worked to get himself faster through the water.

Then monsters came and danced with gigantic leaps along the shore, their double bodies heaving up and down against the stars. Those were the men of Crow's Nest, of course. But they looked like creatures out of a fable, and larger, by far, than human.

Naylor turned his face forward. It would not help his swimming to see the darting fires from the muzzles of the rifles. Therefore he turned, and worked steadily and strongly. His good mustang, in the meantime, had pointed its head a little upstream and was fighting like a Trojan.

A whirling bit of driftwood swept by, its speed showing how well the horse was stemming the current of the stream. And now something like a great water serpent went by, rolling, making a swishing sound in the river. It was not a serpent. It was a great log whose branches had been stripped away far up the course of the river.

Jets of water began to whip across the head and shoulders of Naylor as he swam. He knew they were driven by the impact of the rifle bullets that showered on the stream. He could hear the clangor of the guns. But death by bullets seemed less dreadful than the black coilings of the water in which he floated. Sometimes hands seemed to pluck at him and pull him down. And again and again big logs came hurtling, or low-flying bits of wreckage of one sort or another.

Something approached him with the howling voice of a spirit from among the damned. He made out, at last, a flat bit of wreckage, like the door of a house, and on it a small dog complaining to the stars.

Then, drawn by the shadow of oncoming danger, he glanced to the left and saw peril sweeping toward him straight as an arrow, a gigantic log that lifted a great blank face to beat him down into the dark confusion and death beneath the waters.

CHAPTER X

On the Island

THERE was no way of dodging the log. The mustang, blind with effort, was unable to be controlled. Naylor could not pull himself forward quickly enough to get hand on the reins. All he could do was to watch that looming destruction grow greater and greater, until at the last it struck down the mustang into the depths. Naylor, casting himself free from the tail of the horse, caught at a broken bough that threatened him as with the point of a spear. For the tree trunk was coming down tip first.

As he got his grip on the stub of the branch, the entire log turned rapidly. He was dragged through stifling darkness and brought up on top, where he dragged in a great breath of air and saw the whirling white lines of the stars steady again to single points of fire. Next he saw Duff Gregor in the very act of being overwhelmed by the log. The horse that helped Gregor through the river was struck by the irresistible weight of the log and knocked under.

Bill Naylor thought seven long thoughts in the course of half a second. He cursed himself and his folly—then he twisted his legs around the branch by which he had been lifted to safety, and, stretching out to his full length, he grabbed blindly in the swirl of the current. He grabbed at a shadow and closed a hand on cloth. He pulled hard. The log, slowly turning, gained impetus and dragged him under. Still he maintained his hold. The tree trunk turned very slowly. The effort he was making made it impossible to hold his breath long. He was about to let go his hold when two frantic hands clutched his arm.

"I'm done," he said to himself. "I'm pulled under and gone like a water rat!"

Then the log, slowly, slowly revolving, dragged him up dripping to the starlight once more, and to the incredible mercy of the sweet open air.

Big Duff Gregor came with him and clutched the body of the tree trunk with frantic arms and legs. He groaned and gasped with every breath he drew. There was something so clumsy and desperate, at once, about the way Duff Gregor was clutching at his liberty that Naylor cursed him savagely, and then wanted to laugh.

The log, as though it realized that turning and twisting would no longer get rid of the two human lives that clung to it, stopped rolling. Off to the side, Naylor saw the dark cavalcade of horsemen riding along the bank, still firing.

He lay flat. He gripped the roughness of the bark and hoped the darkness would shelter him, because there was still a spasmodic rifle fire, and he could hear the bullets slash the water. One of the slugs thudded hard into the trunk of the tree inches from his hand.

Before him, Gregor began to sit up straight.

"Lie flat" demanded Naylor.

Duff Gregor lay flat again.

Naylor said: "Lie flat and don't move. Who are you that everybody should make such a fuss to give you a hand? Who are you to be dragged out of trouble? Lie flat and keep flat."

Something urged and swelled in his soul as he saw the big man lie still. Naylor wanted to laugh. To think that he had such control over such a celebrated character as this Duff Gregor, who had the effrontery to play the part of Jim Silver!

Jim Silver? Multiply this rascal by ten and he would still lack ten parts of being a Jim Silver. Size doesn't make the man. Naylor thought greedily of that, taking

61

comfort in his more abbreviated inches. Brains make the man. He himself was no colossus of the world of thought, but he had a brain, just the same. Barry Christian would testify to that.

The rifle fire stopped suddenly, as if a command had been given. The dark silhouettes of the forms along the bank pooled together. Perhaps they had noticed that the horses were gone, and took it for granted that the riders were gone, also. Perhaps this was the end of the pursuit.

A storm was blowing up. It was just conceivable that this might have something to do with influencing the minds of the men of Crow's Nest. Already the stars to the northwest were wiped out. That might be the same storm which had filled the higher valley with surging torrents and started the river flooding. Now it loosed itself suddenly from its birthplace and rolled south and east across the sky. The wind that foreran it blew cold on the wet body of Bill Naylor.

As he looked to the side, he saw that the troop was keeping pace with the drifting of the log. No, now it was turning and scattering. And just before him he saw the loom of the island, like a low-lying bank of mist. To either side of it the bright arcs of the river poured.

"Get ready!" he called. "We're going to swim for the island when we're a little closer."

"Swim nothing," answered Duff Gregor. "Ride the horse that knows the way home. Why not?"

"Don't argue, but do as I tell you!" commanded Naylor. He rejoiced tyrannically that he was able to command.

But still Gregor was arguing.

"We're all right," he said. "Why not stick to the log?"

"Dummy! Because Barry Christian wants to meet us on the island."

"It's a bad play," said Gregor. "They've got the island spotted now. They'll be sure to give it a search."

"They've gone home," answered Naylor.

"Only up the bank to get boats, maybe."

"Hey, d'you know better than Christian?" answered Naylor furiously.

Personally, he would like to meet any man in the world fit to argue a point or make a plan against Barry Christian.

They were close in on the island now. Bill Naylor could see the individual trees come out from the mist of darkness and take shape. There was a little point that had been burned over, and the shapes of the trees were skeletons of horrible grotesqueness. Presently the log began to veer off into the deeper and stronger current.

"Now!" called Naylor, and he dived away from the tree trunk.

He swam strongly, and rejoiced to see that it was easy to make progress across the stream. Looking behind him, he saw Gregor hesitate, then follow with a floundering splash.

"The clumsy fool!" thought Naylor.

Suppose that sharp eyes watched them from the other bank and made out the glimmering of that splash?

But as Naylor gained footing and waded through the softness of the mud through the shallows, and felt again the full weight of his body as he got to turf underfoot, big Duff Gregor came striding up beside him, and the sense of superiority which had been Naylor's vanished at once.

They went on through the trees. The water in their boots made squelching sounds. The forest thickened over them just as the rain commenced. It started with volleyings and crashings the way a heavy downpour in the mountains will often set out. Every time they got out from under the foliage of the evergreens, the strength of the rain whipped and stung their faces with the strength of bullets.

Gregor paused suddenly.

"This is hell," he said.

"Bullets are worse hell," said Naylor. "Or maybe you'd rather have a nice warm jail?"

63

Gregor walked on again, and Bill Naylor disliked him more and more. They came into a natural clearing in what must have been just about the center of the river island. Gregor paused.

"We'll have a fire here," he said, "as long as we have to wait for Christian."

"No fire," directed Bill Naylor. "What's the good of showing people the way to us with a light? What's the good of holding up a light for them to see by?"

"You do as you please," said Gregor. "I'm going to have a fire. No good being saved from jail today to die of pneumonia to-morrow."

"You're all softened up. Or were you ever hard?" asked Naylor.

Gregor turned on him with a savagery of gesture and voice that lighted him up, so to speak.

"I've had your tongue before," said Gregor. "I won't have no more of it. Shut up and keep shut up!"

Naylor drew back—to the proper distance for a full-arm smash. He had a long, whipping, overhand punch that did a lot of damage except to men who were expert boxers. He didn't think that Gregor was much of a boxer, and felt that he might trust that overhand wallop. But Gregor did not press his point. He seemed to think that that shrinking back had meant a good deal. Therefore he turned abruptly away and could be heard tearing up brush. He had found some dead brush; it snapped and crackled under his grasp. A whole herd of horses could hardly have made so much noise.

Where a big tree offered almost perfect shelter from the rain, Gregor built up his small heap of brush for the fire. Soon his voice growled:

"Every match wet. Got any matches, partner?"

"Not to light a fire," answered Naylor.

He was taking off his clothes, preparatory to wringing them as dry as possible. Wet clothes are all right, so long as they're not slopping wet. Clothes only so wet that the heat of the body can dry them out are all right. That is, unless you have to sit still in a wind.

64

"You got a match. Lemme have a match, will you, brother?" pleaded Gregor.

"You big bum," said Naylor. "What kind of a man are you? Jail has gone and softened you all up. Well, here's a match for you. It's on your own hook. I'm not guilty."

"Sure, it's on my own hook," said Gregor. "Nothing but a frog would come to this island on a night like this. We're as safe as if we were on the other side of the mountains."

"Yeah, and that's what you say."

But, finding the oiled silk that carefully wrapped his matches, Naylor handed over the small package. He felt a sulky discontent in surrendering his matches, but when the flame leaped up, yellow-red and cracking, and the first smoke cleared away from the blaze and rolled in low clouds under the wide branches of the tree, he began to change his mind. He finished wringing out his clothes and sat on a stump near the fire in order to empty his boots.

"Yeah, and it ain't so bad, eh?" said Gregor. "Another thing, if Barry Christian's to meet us on the island here, he'll have to have something to guide him, won't he?"

"Yeah? Well, all right," said Naylor. "The only thing is, I've always gone on the idea that there's nothing safer than playing safe."

"Aw, we're all right," insisted Gregor. "I'll take the responsibility. It'll be all on me."

"You won't take the bullets, though. They won't ask you which way they ought to travel."

"Who'll shoot at you?" cried Gregor suddenly. "Who'll even think of you? It's me they're after."

Bill Naylor lowered his head and looked from under the darkness of his brows at his companion. It was a big figure of a man that he saw, with really magnificent shoulders, and the head well-placed on them. The face was handsome, too. There had not been enough jail to fade all the sun-brown off the skin.

More than once Naylor had seen pictures of Jim

65

Silver, and he could understand how it might be that people would mistake this man for the famous fighter. There were even the two spots of gray over the temples, like incipient horns. They gave a sinister touch to the figure of the big fellow. He was stripping off his clothes now, and his body was big with muscle. But it was not quite the effect that one would expect to get from seeing the real Jim Silver stripped. There was not the same easy and stringy flow of muscles that gave speed to the bulk when it was in action. It seemed to Naylor that there was a touch of weakness about the mouth of this man, also.

"All right," said Naylor. "It's you that they're after, all right. I know that."

He got out his tobacco pouch, so well wrapped and waterproofed that not a drop had touched the contents. He loaded his short pipe, whose stem had been worried off to little more than a half of its original length, with a new hold for the teeth whittled into the hard rubber. He began to smoke, sucking hard at the tobacco until the flame was well spread and the coal tamped down.

"Got any papers?" asked the other.

"No."

"Can't I have a smoke, then? Lemme have a whiff, will you, partner?"

There was a slight whine in the voice. The lips of Naylor twitched.

He removed the pipe from his mouth. He prided himself on a certain number of delicacies. Now he took out a clean handkerchief. It was soaked with the river water, of course, but that didn't matter. He used it to cleanse the mouthpiece of the pipe, and then handed it over, stem first.

Gregor grabbed it with a greedy hand and began to draw down great whiffs of the smoke. He started talking, his enunciation biting the exhalation of smoke to pieces.

"Rotten strong stuff you smoke," he said. "Rotten cheap stuff!"

Naylor said nothing. He registered the bad taste of this remark and said nothing whatever. Things like this helped him to place his companion. There was no use arguing about such a point. Except on a Monday morning, when one wants to get warmed up for a long, hard week.

"Yeah, it's strong," he drawled finally.

He watched Gregor consuming the pipe load rapidly. After a long time Gregor asked:

"What's your name?"

"Naylor."

"Which Naylor?"

"Bill Naylor."

Gregor chuckled.

"You don't like it, eh?"

"That's all right," said Gregor.

Naylor looked slowly away. The jump of the firelight gave him view of long vistas among the brown tree trunks. Shapes seemed to move with the toss and the swing of the fire.

"I dunno," he said as a bit of water was shaken from a bough above and went down his neck. "I dunno. Maybe it's not all right."

"Don't get the bulldog up, Shorty," cautioned Gregor, lifting a threatening finger.

Then a deep, soft voice, close to them said.

"Hands up, please! Stick them right up, boys."

CHAPTER XI

Jim Silver

THE mind of Bill Naylor slashed through several reflections and one great regret as he heard that voice. He looked straight at Duff Gregor and saw the shock strike the big fellow like a bullet. It paralyzed Gregor. It froze him in mid-gesture, so to speak.

"Right up, friends," said the soft, deep voice.

It seemed to Naylor like the sort of a voice that one would expect from the spirit of the island, half obscured and dark. There was music in it that went with the sound of the storm. And then the wind, following after, screeched suddenly through the near-by treetops.

Gregor groaned.

Naylor shoved up his hands slowly. Firelight is not good light to shoot by. If he took a dive backward, rolling on the ground, he could get himself into a tangle of brush, and from that behind the trees, and it would take very snappy and straight shooting to get him. Not every man can do much with a revolver in the daylight. Not one in a thousand is any good at night.

"If one of you makes a quick start, I'll have to nail him," said the voice of the unseen man. "I mean you, Shorty, if that's your name! Gregor, get the hands right up over your head and try to grab that branch of the tree."

Gregor was obedient. Bill Naylor decided that this was not the time to take chances—not just now. For there was no hysterical yell in the throat of the unknown man. There was no strain of excitement. There was simply the businesslike intonation of one who is in a familiar situation.

Then, as Naylor got his hands high, straight toward him out of the shadows stepped a big man whose wet slicker glistened like polished steel. He had a gun in either hand, and he held those guns low, about the level of his stomach. He held them with the careless mastery of one who knows his tools. He looked like a brother of big Duff Gregor, an older and a better-made brother. There was more in the shoulders and less in the hips. There was more in the flesh, and more under the flesh, so to speak.

And all at once Naylor cried out as realization struck him sick: "Jim Silver!"

Gregor seemed to feel the words in the pit of the stomach. He gasped, as he bent forward with a jerk: "Silver? Jim Silver?" And he twisted his head and stood there agape. "It's Jim Silver!"

"I suppose it was in the books for me to meet you one day," said Silver. "Straighten up and keep those hands high, Gregor."

A faint, moaning sound came from the lips of Gregor, and Naylor thought it was like the whining of a young puppy exposed to weather such as this.

"Both of you face away from me," said Silver. "Then you can put your hands down and shell out your guns. Move your hands slowly. I hope nobody's going to be hurt."

There was a quiet irony about this. Naylor made no mistakes. He deliberately, slowly, faced around, and then pulled out his pair of guns and dropped them one by one to the ground. Gregor had a gun, too, and got rid of it.

"Is that all boys?" asked Silver.

"Yes," said Naylor.

And Gregor added: "Every scrap of everything."

"Get back close to the fire," said Silver. "You're cold. Start in dressing. I don't have to tell you that I'm watching all the time for queer moves."

69

Naylor obeyed and began to dress. He was cold, and shuddering a little. He could see that Gregor was so frightened that he was almost incapable of getting the well-wrung clothes back on his body.

When Naylor was dressed, he said: "Well, Silver? What happens next?"

He was surprised to hear Silver say: "I don't know. Just what do you suggest? What's your name, again?"

"Naylor. Bill Naylor."

"I think I've heard that name. What do you do?"

Naylor canted his head a little. It never had been very hard to face the lawmen, no matter what they knew about his record. It was not so good to tell things to this man, somehow. It made him feel a little homesick, uneasy in the spirit.

"I live on my face," said Naylor.

"What do you mean by that?"

"You think over what you've heard about me, and you'll understand."

"You mean that you live by your wits?"

"What there are of them," admitted Naylor.

Something happened to the gun that was occupied in covering him. It got a little steadier; it came to life; it took on a certain eager sentience.

"What's your record?" asked Silver.

"Oh, anything you like. I've run chinks over the border and I've been a stick-up artist. A lot of things in between. Why?"

"Well," murmured Silver. "Well, I don't know. And on the road you and Gregor became friends?"

Naylor grunted.

Silver maintained a long silence. He sighed, at last, and said:

"I thought that Gregor was a rat. I was wrong. No man that has a friend like you, Naylor, is a rat."

Naylor waited for the new qualification. There might be things lower than and worse than rats. But Silver was not supposed to be a fellow who scattered insults. There was something in the air that was strange.

"I've been in the jail in Crow's Nest," said Silver. "I know what it means to get out of it. Taxi got me out one night. It was a hard job. And if you've taken out Duff Gregor, you have brains and nerve, Naylor. That's all."

Naylor saw how the wind was blowing, but he could not believe his eyes and his ears. Big Duff Gregor had finished dressing. He stood straight and stiff by the fire, holding out his hands to the blaze rather as if he wanted to make a shadow for his face than to get warmth into his blood.

"Silver," he began, "what I want to say is that that other deal——"

"Don't!" said Silver. "Don't say it. I'd rather not talk with you, Gregor. I'd rather not hear from you."

Gregor's teeth clicked together in the ecstasy of his fear. He spoke not a word more. And a strange shame suffused the very soul of Naylor as he saw that Silver felt that this jail break had been managed by him, by Bill Naylor, simply because of the friendship that he bore for the big man.

Silver said: "I've wanted to know that Gregor was in jail, safely behind the bars. Perhaps another day I'll be trying to put him where I've always thought that he belongs. But there's nothing in the world as great as friendship. You've done a big thing, Naylor. You've done such a big thing that I'm not going to spoil it for you. Not to-night."

Gradually Bill Naylor understood. He could not take in the whole thing at once. He had to feel his way through the idea little by little. Friendship is a sacred thing. According to the understanding of Silver, Naylor had done the greatest thing that can be done; he had offered his life for that of another; he had done it through sheer affection.

What would Silver feel if he knew that the money of Barry Christian had organized this whole deal?

Other things went through the mind of Bill Naylor. He could see that we judge others by what is inside us. That was how Jim Silver was judging Naylor—by what

71

Silver would have been capable of in the same circumstances. He was judging Naylor, too, by what "Taxi" had done for him on that other, that famous night when Taxi took his friend out of the Crow's Nest jail, through the lynching mob.

Something swelled in the throat of Naylor and tried to speak. He had to choke it down. It was a crazy impulse to confess the truth. It was an insane feeling that he could not bear to be misunderstood, even for the better, by this man Jim Silver.

But there was Duff Gregor, standing straight and stiff, as though his backbone were a rod of ice. One word of the truth about affairs would ruin Gregor. One word connecting his jail break with Barry Christian would be the destruction of Gregor.

On what a mine of danger Silver himself was standing, thought Naylor, with his greatest enemy restored to the world from death! Ignorance blindfolded Jim Silver. Perhaps that ignorance which he could not help would permit Christian to steal up and deliver the fatal blow.

Such a rage of contrasting emotions as troubled Naylor at this moment never had disturbed him before.

Then he heard men from the distant calling, answering one another faintly. Big Gregor heard the sounds, too, and started violently.

"It's my duty," said Silver, "to hold you both here until the men from Crow's Nest come up and get the pair of you. Well, I'm not going to be true to my duty. They're going to go over this little island with a fine-tooth comb. There's no way you can get through them. I saw them scattering out to encircle the place. There must be fifty of them. But—well, suppose you drop into this bit of brush right here by the fire. I'll throw my slicker over the brush to keep it in shadow. I'll freshen the fire to make the flames dazzle 'em a little. Here, take these guns. We don't want 'em in the way."

72

CHAPTER XII

The Posse

BILL NAYLOR found himself crouched in the brush with the shadow of the slicker covering him. When he stooped his head lower, he could look out beneath the skirt of the big rubberized garment and see the firelit scene.

Jim Silver had said only one thing in conclusion: "You've got your guns. Don't use them. You've only got them in trust while I try to handle this crowd."

And the voice of Gregor had whispered in savage answer: "Yeah, the first shot I'd take would be at you, you——"

The whispered curses were things that Naylor could not believe. There is such a thing as gratitude in this world. There has to be. Otherwise everything falls to pieces; there is nothing that a man can catch hold of. Substance turns to air unless there is gratitude.

For instance, Barry Christian must feel gratitude for what had been done for him by Naylor. He must recollect that Naylor had picked him out of death in the river; he must remember that the fortune in his hands at the present moment had been placed there by Naylor at the cost of hair-raising peril endured. And again, it was for the sake of Barry Christian, not of Barry's money, that Bill Naylor had met the jailbird Gregor and endured the peril of the river chase.

Those were the things that kept hunting through the mind of Naylor as he crouched in the brush while the new fuel was heaped on the fire by Jim Silver and the flames rushed upward, throwing shuddering waves of

73

light through the green-and-brown obscurity of the trees. That is what the human soul is like—a dark, entangled jungle except where human faith and trust and affection illumine it. But such light could never penetrate the mind of Duff Gregor, Naylor felt.

Gregor was ready at this moment, at the first touch of danger, to crash a bullet through the heart of the man who had just spared him. And how great was the weight of the past to keep Silver from sparing Gregor. Next to Barry Christian, who was there in the world that Silver had so many reasons for hating?

It was a frightful turmoil that these things made in the mind of Naylor as he reflected upon them. He had the vast picture of Barry Christian in his mind's eye, a huge brain, a mighty power, endless in resource and craft. That man was his friend. He had bought the friendship of Barry Christian by such acts as he never had performed for any other human being in all of his days. But Barry Christian was a force all for evil. And here was another man greater than Christian, more powerful in brain and in body, but weakened only because he could not help having faith and trust in the goodness of his fellow man. And all the force and the weight of Silver was on the side of good.

Well, it was not strange, thought Naylor, that there were people ready to die for Jim Silver!

For his own part—well, Naylor was a crook by taste, by life, and by training. Therefore he would cling to Barry Christian. But——

He had reached that point in his reflections when the noise of the men of Crow's Nest came close to the place. They came stamping through the brush. The waves of their lantern light fought with the softer, wider waves of the firelight. They were scanning the trees and hunting every hole as they closed in. Then, with a sudden rush, they were through the trees, on one side of the clearing.

"We've got him!" yelled voices. "Hey! We've got Gregor! Up with your hands, Gregor! Up with 'em!"

74

Gregor shuddered violently. Naylor looked out and saw the men swarming toward Jim Silver, who stood with his hands raised, very calm, saying:

"All right, boys!"

That reminded Naylor of what he had heard—that Silver was helpless against other honest men. That was why he had almost been pulled down by the Crow's Nest mob once before.

They went in at Jim Silver with a savage eagerness, till one of them shouted:

"Wait a minute! It's not Gregor! It's the real Jim Silver!"

"You fool," said another, "Silver's gone away. This *is* Gregor. It's gotta be Gregor!"

"It ain't Gregor. It's Jim Silver. Look at the scars on his face."

"Gregor made up once before with them same scars."

"He ain't had time to make up with 'em. Besides, it ain't the same face. It's Silver. Jim, I'm sorry we rushed you."

"That's all right," said Jim Silver.

"If it's Silver, where's Parade?" asked another voice.

Silver whistled. And out of the darkness beyond the fire, in the direction from which the rest of the men of Crow's Nest were hurrying toward the shouting, sounded a loud neighing. Brush crackled, and Naylor, his face close to the ground, peering out beneath the flap of the slicker, saw a great golden chestnut stallion leap into the circle of the firelight and rush for his master. Other men were in the way. They scattered with a yell of fear from the striking hoofs of the big horse. And now Parade stood at the side of Jim Silver, snorting, tossing his head, defying danger like one who had long been intimate with it.

Horses had always been to Naylor mere means of locomotion. Suddenly he saw that a horse could be to a man like a throne to a king.

Newcomers of the Crow's Nest men, wet and panting with their laboring through the marshes, scratched and stung by breaking through the dense brush of the island, now came blundering into view with excited faces.

Gradually they realized that it was not the man they had hunted for.

Sheriff Dick Williams suddenly appeared, soaked, bedraggled, looking like a man who had risen newly from a sick bed. He went up to Silver and held out his hand.

"Are we shaking, Jim?" he asked. "Or do you keep hard feelings about the way Crow's Nest treated you in the old days?"

Silver took the hand willingly.

"I'm not such a fool," he said, and then took his stand right by the coat which covered the two fugitives. It was not the slicker; it was the great name and reputation of Silver that sheltered the pair, Naylor felt.

"Gregor got away," said the sheriff. "I won't have the reputation of a yellow dog in the county. You and Taxi open the jail like an old tin can; and now Gregor gets hold of keys somehow and simply unlocks three doors and walks out while I'm forward in my office. Gregor, and there was another gent with him—the gent that had horses waiting. It's bad business for me, Jim!"

Silver nodded. Naylor, staring cautiously up into the face of the sheriff, wondered at the man. A few days ago he had been as straight and as honest as any man in the mountains. For his straightness and his courage he had been proverbial. Well, he was a bought man now—and he looked ten years older. He was bought, and Barry Christian's money had turned the trick.

"Every man has a price," Christian had said—every man except Jim Silver. But that was not true, either. Silver had been bought and paid for on this night. A mistaken kindness and sentiment had undone his good intentions and made him harbor a pair of rascals.

The men of Crow's Nest seemed to forget about the man hunt that they had been engaged in.

A big fellow said: "Hey, Jim Silver; dog-gone me but it does me good to see you ag'in."

"Thanks, Harry," said Silver.

"But Gregor and the other are gone. We sure seen 'em get onto the island, all right. Seen anything of 'em, Jim?"

Silver said nothing. Another man cried, on the heel of the words of Harry:

"If he'd seen 'em, wouldn't he 'a' grabbed 'em? If he'd seen Gregor living, we'd be looking at Gregor dead right now. Ain't you got any sense, Harry?"

"We'll have to scatter out, boys," said the sheriff. "We'll have to get across on the far side of the island. The current's a lot shallower and weaker there. We can manage it, all right."

"I'm wet enough for one night," said Harry, leading one half of the sentiment with his loud voice. "Hey, Jim, what's brought you back again to Crow's Nest?"

"I'm not in Crow's Nest, Harry," said Silver in his deep and quiet voice.

"Aye, but ain't you on your way? Tell us, Silver—you aint' on your way to a wedding, are you?"

There was no answer from Silver. One of the other men said:

"Shut up, Harry. Don't be such a loud mouth!"

Others grinned. Their grins were brief. It seemed that the respect in which they held Silver would not permit them to do otherwise than stare at the man with a consuming awe.

They began to divide into two parties. Half were returning to Crow's Nest. Others would push on behind the sheriff, who was reminding them that the two fugitives were not mounted. If there were any luck, the pair would be picked up before the night ended. At any rate, there was no use in wasting time on this spot, since the island already had been searched.

"Are you coming on with us, Jim?" asked one.

"I'm staying here—for a while," said Jim Silver.

Then the two parties separated, a few not too cheer-

77

ful insults being hurled by the resolute followers of the sheriff after the heads of the weaker members who were returning home to warm beds.

The sheriff shook hands with Silver in farewell.

He said in a quiet voice: "Remember, Jim, we want you in Crow's Nest. We're not the only town that wants you, but no other town owes you so much. There's no other crowd that you can count on so much, eh?"

"Thanks," said Silver. "You look sick, sheriff."

"Do I?" said the sheriff in a startled voice.

"You look as though you'd gotten up from a sick bed."

"I'm all right," said the sheriff. "Right as a trivet."

"And the boy?" said Silver.

"Why," murmured the sheriff, "he ain't so good."

"I heard that he needed a change of air," said Silver. "I got word about it, and, as a matter of fact, Williams, I remembered that I have a good bit of cash that's not working, and I wondered if you'd let me help you out with the boy."

"You?" said the sheriff in a groaning voice. "You help me out, Jim?"

And he turned suddenly and fled as if wild wolves were after him. But Naylor understood. If the sheriff had waited one more day, he would have had honest money instead of a bribe to use.

Perhaps on that night, thought Naylor, the great event was not the freeing of Gregor or the great-hearted kindness of Jim Silver; it was the personal tragedy of the sheriff who had sold himself at the very moment when honest help was coming toward him.

It was a very queer thing. The queerest of all was that Naylor did not feel like laughing about it!

CHAPTER XIII

Surprised

As THE men of Crow's Nest scattered, Silver began to pace up and down beside the fire, careless of whether or not the rain came rattling down on his head and shoulders. After a time, when not a voice could be heard out of the distance, he said:

"Come out, boys."

They came out into the firelight.

"You made a flock of fools of 'em," cried Duff Gregor. "That was the slickest that I ever seen, Jim! That was a beauty! Kind of too bad that they ain't ever goin' to know what a lot of fools you made of 'em!"

Silver looked straight and hard at him.

"Perhaps they will know, one day," said Silver. "Perhaps they'll know when you're caught up again, Gregor."

"Me? The gang that ever catches me is goin' to have nothing but dead meat to handle, lemme tell you!" answered Duff Gregor, striking one hand into the palm of the other.

Silver looked steadily at him and said nothing. Bill Naylor, a little shamed by this desperate boast of Gregor, bit his lip and stared at the fire.

"It was the best job," said Gregor, "that I ever seen, and it saved my hide. Here's my hand, Silver."

Silver looked down at the proffered hand and shook his head. Gradually the smile of Gregor froze, and his hand fell away. It seemed to Naylor one of the most terrible things that he had ever seen.

Silver said, more gently than ever: "We'd better not

shake hands, Gregor. There are too many things that we don't know about one another. Maybe I'm doing the worst thing of my life in letting you go. But Bill Naylor has done a job that I wouldn't want to spoil."

The shudder caused by that speech was still working up and down the spine of Bill Naylor long after they were off the island, long after they had forded the narrower arm of the Kendal River and had floundered such miles through wind and mud that their clothes were beginning to grow dry on their tired bodies. He felt that he would far rather have had heavy leaden slugs tearing through his body than to have listened to the speech of Jim Silver.

But all that Duff Gregor did about it at the time was to fall silent. And all that he did about it now was to curse Jim Silver and all of his kind.

Naylor stopped him suddenly by halting in a lull of the storm and saying:

"Well, except for the way Jim Silver acted, the pair of us would be on the way back to jail—or dead—by now."

Gregor had to consider this remark for a time before he ventured: "Look here, Bill. You beginning to think that Silver's the right kind of a gent?"

Naylor could not answer this. For if Silver was "the right kind of a gent," then the entire life of Naylor was thrown away. No, Silver could not be "the right kind of a gent." It was Barry Christian who must serve as the ideal.

They followed the course which Christian had prescribed for them if they did not meet on the island. He had told Bill Naylor to keep on a certain trail until he reached the remains of an old ranch. The ranch house itself was gone to ruin, and the sheds were sinking in corruption; but there remained the huge barn that had once housed hundreds of tons of wild hay against the winter season of scarcity. It was far into the night when at last those weary travelers saw the roof and the shoulders of the barn break across the smoothly running lines of the hills. Big Duff Gregor had been

80

cursing the journey long before they reached this goal.

As the barn arose, huge and black, close to them, Bill Naylor whistled the signal which had been agreed upon. A moment later the whistle of Barry Christian gave answer, and Naylor could have groaned with relief.

As they came up they saw the vague outlines of Christian standing beside the big sliding door that closed one end of the barn. His voice gave them greeting:

"Hello, Gregor. Well done, Bill!"

He shook hands with Gregor, who exclaimed:

"They gave us hell! We needed faster horses than that pair."

"You should have pulled out without being seen," answered Christian.

"It was bad luck that gave 'em a glimpse of me," said Gregor, "and after that the whole town came on the run after us. They came like so many devils."

"They thought they were running *after* two devils," said Christian. "You two are fagged. Well, we can spend the rest of the night here—until the gray of the morning. By that time we ought to get away into the hills. Come in here and you can turn in."

He showed the way into the barn. There were still heaps of the old hay on the floor, and behind a partition in a corner of the big building, Gregor and Naylor simply burrowed into the hay and prepared to close their eyes.

Christian sat down on his heels near by and talked to them for a moment. He had his horse hobbled out at a little distance from the barn, he said. One of them could ride it when they started the march in the morning; for his part, he would be glad enough to stretch his legs, walking. They would not have to go far into the hills before they would come to places where they could buy good horses. Because this was a district where the old days of Barry Christian were remembered, and where men would be glad to see them return—days when big amounts of ready cash could be secured in reward for very small acts of service done to the great outlaw or to his men.

"I showed myself to one man," said Christian. "He thought I was a ghost come to haunt him, at first; but afterward he seemed to be glad that I was around. We are going to start something in this same neck of the woods. I'm going to line the pockets of you fellows with gold!"

Gregor groaned with relief and comfort as the hay pressed close to him the warmth of his own body.

"We been through a lot to-night," he said. "We'll talk about the next job in the morning. You know what we've been through? We've been through Jim Silver."

The silence of Barry Christian was a throbbing thing that Naylor felt through the darkness. Then his voice, strangely flat, said:

"Silver again?"

"Silver again," said Gregor, and told the story in some detail. He ended by cursing Silver for not being willing to shake hands. But Christian began to laugh. There was a snarl in his laughter.

"That's his weak side. That's where he's a fool," said Christian. "One of these days I'll work on that weak side of his and get him down. I begin to know how to handle him. Make an appeal of a certain sort to him and he can't resist it. Here's Bill Naylor, half his life in prison, and on the way to join me; but Jim Silver lets the pair of you go because he takes it for granted that Bill has been a hero and helped you out because he's your best friend. The poor fool! He doesn't realize that my money walked Bill out of the town. Why, it makes me laugh!

"And Silver hears that the honest sheriff has a sick child, and he comes all the way back to Crow's Nest to lend him money, eh? Well, the honest sheriff has money of a different sort, right now—and he's going to repay it with his blood. I'm not through bleeding him. But what pleases me is the fact that Jim Silver

82

can be bamboozled like this. That's why I laugh. And that's why I'm going to have him down one of these days. No fool can stand up against me and keep on winning!"

There was truth in that remark, and Bill Naylor felt it. No mere fool could stand up against Barry Christian. Not even if he had all the skill, strength, and courage in the world. He could not succeed against Christian so long as he showed a really weak side, and that was what Silver was indicating. He was too corrupted by belief in the natural goodness of human nature. He could trust, actually, to a rogue like Bill Naylor, jailbird.

And yet perhaps there was something in the heart of Bill Naylor that had been touched more deeply than he himself knew. He closed his eyes and found himself picturing again the scene by the camp fire among the trees, and the formidable shape of Silver, glistening in the wet slicker. He could remember every tone of the man's voice. He could remember what Silver had said about friendship as the most sacred thing in the world.

Perhaps it was.

Naylor, opening his eyes suddenly, stared up at the blank and whirling darkness. Suppose, he thought, that the friendship of such a man as Jim Silver should come to him? What would he, Naylor, be willing to do for the sake of it when he had been willing to do so much even to be esteemed a man by Barry Christian, who always sneered at such ideas as those of friendship?

According to Christian, the mainspring of our actions is the desire for profit, and he had built up his formidable gangs in the trust that he, Christian, was more profitable to them than any other man could be. But still there was something working in the heart of Naylor.

Then, with a great, screeching voice, the sliding door at the end of the barn was thrust open. Men entered, and wide waves of lantern light washed through the blackness of the interior!

CHAPTER XIV

A Big Deal

THE characteristics of the three appeared in that instant in good part. Duff Gregor came to his feet with a hissing outgo of his frightened breath. Naylor got to one knee, with a gun ready in his hand. And Barry Christian said, not even using a whisper, so perfectly was he aware of the way sound would travel:

"They're not looking for us. There are only three. And they're holding lights for us to shoot by, if we want to take them in hand. Steady, boys. By thunder, I think I know two of 'em. I *do* know two of 'em!"

He had out a pair of guns. The glimmer of them in those famous hands made Naylor feel that the lives of the three strangers could be wiped away with a mere gesture.

The three were composed of a tall man in the prime of life, with very nervous movements of head and hand; a big, bulky fellow with so much stomach that it was certain that he would be uncomfortable on horseback, and another fellow of average size. He and the tall fellow carried lanterns. One of these was hung up against the wall of the barn. The fat man sat down on the hay cross-legged and made a cigarette. All three of those tossed aside wet slickers.

Barry Christian was saying in a whisper to his companions: "The fat man, Pudge Wayler. The tall man, Pokey. The other's new; the first two used to work for me. This is something worth while."

84

It was in fact something worth while, as almost the first words of the conversation revealed.

For "Pudge" Wayler was saying: "All right, Mr. Rooney. This ought to be a safe enough place even for an express clerk to talk in."

Rooney walked in an irregular circle toward the fading borders of the lantern light. Then he exclaimed:

"It's a rotten hard business for me, Wayler. You fellows have the law on your backs, anyway, but I have forty years of going straight behind me. Let me tell you this right now. If I go through with the deal, you'll have to pay me for the forty years."

"Sure, sure," said the fat man. He took off his sombrero and ran his hand over his fat, shining bald head and his face. "Don't worry about that, old son. You'll get your split."

"How big a split do you make it?" asked Rooney.

"That depends on how big the job is," said Wayler.

"How big?" demanded Rooney. "Are you fellows such green hands that you have to be told what it means to stop an overland express train and get at the money safe with two express guards on hand to protect it?"

"Listen," said "Pokey," making a nervous gesture with both hands. "Didn't I tell you that we used to work for Barry Christian? Does that mean that we're dumb? We mean—how much is going to be in the safe?"

"Three hundred and fifty thousand, if there's a penny."

Pokey did not exclaim. He merely turned and looked down at Wayler with a smile.

Pudge Wayler said: "Well, that's a neat little haul. What slice do you want?"

"One third," said Rooney.

"Hello, hello!" said Wayler.

"Wait a minute," urged Pokey with polite sarcasm. "You don't understand what he means, Pudge. He means that he tips off the lay to us, and then you and me hold up the train, kill the guards, blow the safe, and get

85

out the haul. That's all we have to do, and that makes it a three-cornered split."

"I'm not a fool!" said Rooney. "I know that you'll have to have half a dozen good men in on the deal with you."

"And still you want a whole third for yourself?" asked Pudge Wayler.

"I want a whole third," said Rooney. "I'm the one who spots the train that takes the shipment. Otherwise you fellows would never be able to put your hand on the right train. You'd have your trouble for almost nothing. I get a third or I don't go through."

Wayler and Pokey consulted one another with silent eyes. They said nothing, and Rooney went on:

"Another thing. This has to be a right job. You can't just grab the safe and then run for it. I want the whole list of passengers searched the way a regular train robbery would be run off. Otherwise it'll be too plain that somebody has tipped you off about the cash shipment."

"That's true," said Pudge Wayler. "That's sense. But it's a tricky job, sometimes, handling a long list of passengers. It takes time, and some of those hombres may have guns and know how to use 'em."

"I'm not saying that it's easy," Rooney assured him. "I'm just telling you what has to be done if you fellows are going to work with me."

"The boy is hungry, and he knows just what he wants to eat," answered Pokey satirically.

"I've told you the facts. You can wrangle them to suit yourselves," said Rooney. "Tell me short and straight: Do you play the game my way, or not at all?"

"Wait a minute, Rooney," said Pudge Wayler. "You got the wrong idea. I can see what's put you off. You've had the idea that train robbers are kind of benevolent brotherhoods. You got an idea that fellows that rob trains are just doing it for the sake of getting a little fun. And then they give away the hard cash to the gents with the great brains that sit in offices in town and polish mahogany desks with their heels. Is that the picture you're drawin' of us?"

Rooney had the grace to laugh. The other two laughed, also, but very shortly.

"All right, boys," said Rooney. "I know what you mean. But you're the fishermen with the rods and lines, and I'm the fellow who hooks the fish on under the water. That's why I get the big split. There are not five men in the outfit that could tell you the train that shipment goes on."

Wayler nodded. "There's not five men," he said, "that can tell you how straight those guards on the train are going to be able to shoot. And I don't have to stand twice to make a shadow."

"I know," said Rooney. "That's another thing that I've got on my mind. I'm sending those two poor devils to their death. I'm doing about the rottenest trick that any human being can do. And I'm going to be paid for it or I won't go through."

Pokey barked out, his voice suddenly high and shrill: "You go to the devil, then! I got a mind to bash in your face for you!"

Rooney made a quick, jerking step to the rear, and a little bulldog revolver appeared in his hand.

"All right, boys," he said. "If that's the way you feel about it, it's just too bad. And the deal quits right here. I'll say so long to you and go home."

"I don't know," said Pudge Wayler, who had a big Colt lying out on his knee the instant that Rooney made a move. "I don't know about all of this. You got some information that we want. I dunno that you're so sure of leaving before we have that news out of you."

"No," yelled Pokey. "You can name that train, and you're goin' to do it!"

He, also, had a gun in his hand, and slipped off to the side so as to take Rooney between two fires.

The express-company man seemed perfectly at home in the situation. He was at least not the sort to be bluffed. He said: "Back up, Pokey. Mind you, you may

87

get me, but I'll get one of you first. And you're the man, Wayler. You're the easiest target, and I've got you in my eye. Tell Pokey to back up!"

His voice had lowered. He seemed preoccupied, and the preoccupation was plainly with his gun.

Here Barry Christian arose and moved forward through the gloom. He called out:

"Steady, boys. We'll have a new deal here."

Pokey and Rooney stopped moving. Pudge Wayler got to one fat knee. And Duff Gregor moved with Naylor at the shoulders of their chief.

"Who's there?" called Rooney.

"A man you all may need," said Christian.

"It's the voice of Barry Christian!" yelled Wayler, jumping to his feet with surprising lightness.

"You fool!" answered the steady Rooney. "I know—the whole world knows—that Christian's dead in the Kendal River."

Barry Christian walked straight on into the lantern light. He said:

"Hello, Pudge. Hello, Pokey. Glad to see you, Rooney, in——"

There was a wild yell from Pokey. He threw both arms high over his head and bolted for the door of the barn. He issued from it, his screeching of terror trailing behind him like blown flames behind a torch.

"Let him go," said Christian. "He'll think it over and come back to see."

"It's a lucky thing," said Rooney, "that I didn't mix myself up with that sort of a yellow hound."

"Steady, Mr. Rooney," answered Christian. "Pokey is the sort that fights like a wild cat, but he's not used to ghosts."

Big Pudge Wayler had put up his gun, and now he came forward with both hands stretched out before him, and his eyes popping in his fat, pale face. He actually grasped Christian with both hands, and then groaned out:

"It's Barry—and no——"

88

He paused there, too overcome for speech. Christian seemed a little moved by this reception, for he slapped the shoulder of the fat man and answered:

"There's not enough water in the world to soak me all the way through, Pudge. You boys get to know one another. Here's Bill Naylor, who pulled me out of the river. Here's Duff Gregor, who stood Crow's Nest on its head and nearly split the better part of a million with me. They've heard your names. You fellows all seemed to be trying to advertise one another. Shake hands and get acquainted."

They shook hands all around—all except Rooney, who preferred to keep his gun out and scowl at the strangers.

He was a regular bulldog type, with eyes buried under deep brows and a square, wide, projecting jaw.

"You're not Barry Christian," he said. "This is a plant of some sort. Christian went down the Kendal River."

"Look at me again, Rooney," said Christian. "You must have seen pictures of me. I can trust the newspapers to have spread pictures of me all over the land. Look at me again, and you'll recognize me."

He stood close to the lantern that hung on the wall, and Rooney suddenly nodded.

"I've got to believe my eyes," he admitted.

"This is a lucky meeting, I hope, for both of us," said Christian, and, walking forward, he held out his hand.

Rooney hesitated only an instant. Then, with a short, barking laugh, he put up his gun and accepted Christian's hand.

"Except for the way Pokey acted," he said, "I think I'd still take it for a hoax. But Pokey wasn't on a stage when he ran out of the barn. Christian, what do you know of this deal I've been talking over?"

"Only what I heard in this barn. I've been busy, lately, getting Gregor out of jail. We had to look sharp. His trial commences tomorrow."

Once more admiration of the great criminal overwhelmed Naylor. After all, what other man would have

89

been so true to his follower? What other man, in the first place, would even have dreamed of bribery in the case of the honest sheriff in Crow's Nest?

And now, at the first turn of the cards, it seemed that Christian was about to step into another big deal.

"Aye," said Rooney, "I've read the papers about Duff Gregor. He's the one that filled the shoes of Jim Silver for a while. Well, that was even a bigger deal than the one I've been talking about."

"Why, Rooney," said Christian, "we can't always talk in terms of millions. We have to pick up the chicken feed when we're pinched."

He chuckled.

"Sit down in a circle," he advised, "and we'll go over the deal man to man."

They sat down, and Christian took direction at once, saying:

"First we have to settle with you, Pudge. Do you want me to come in—with Gregor and Naylor?"

"Want you?" cried Wayler. "What else do I want as much? Want you? Why, we've got to have you!"

"Thanks," said Christian. "And you, Rooney. Will you do business with me?"

Rooney smiled. "Of course I will," said he. "The only reason I opened up with the others was because I knew they'd once been your men. This is what I call a lucky meeting."

"Then," said Christian, "we have to settle on your share first of all. You want a third, and that's just twice as much as you'll get from me."

"Then the thing's off," Rooney said.

"It certainly is," answered Christian. "I have to think about this deal, and I have to think about a hundred other deals that may be in the future. It's a matter of business policy. If I pay you a third for information, I'll have to pay the next man a half or two thirds."

Rooney stared at him.

"You're a sensible man," Christian said. "You're forty years old. You haven't made as much money as you

90

think you need. You want a bigger income. And this is your way of getting it. I'll offer you fifty thousand if there's over three hundred thousand in the clean-up."

"Not enough," growled Rooney.

"It's three thousand dollars a year," said Barry Christian. "Look at it in that light. It's two hundred and fifty dollars a month. What would you do to have your salary increased by that much?"

Rooney was silent, contemplative.

"Besides," said Christian, "you know that when you work with me you are with a man who will cover you up. I'll take care of you. I'll see that you're protected. If the law hounds get on your track in any way, it won't be a leak through me. And I'll help you when the pinch comes."

"I know your reputation, Christian," said Rooney, nodding. "When you make a deal, you follow it up and give—the good will of the firm!"

He laughed briefly.

"Well?" said Christian.

"Well," Rooney muttered, "now that you're on the job, I suppose that it'll go through. I'll work with you at the cut rate, Christian. Here's my hand on it."

CHAPTER XV

The Townsend Ranch

ONE name and a memory beside it began to fill the world of Bill Naylor. The name was Barry Christian; the memory was Jim Silver. Naylor wanted to keep Christian in the foreground and push Silver into the distance. Christian stood for everything that Naylor

91

had wanted to be. Silver stood for everything that he felt he could not be. That was the difference between the name and the memory.

Naylor took a very personal pleasure in the way in which Christian began to run things. He took a pleasure in the "pull" which Christian had.

When they went back into the hills to get horses, provisions, and call in new members to the gang, wherever Christian appeared, things were easy. The party journeyed to a small ranch back in the hills. When they came into sight of it, Christian took Naylor with him, left the rest to camp among some trees, and rode down to bargain for horses.

They found the owner of the ranch busily fencing in a small corral near his house. A girl with a flopping straw hat and a suit of faded blue overalls was helping at the work.

As the pair of them came up, Christian called the man Townsend and hailed the girl as Sally. They made a great fuss. They came running over, Townsend trailing a crowbar with which he had been tamping the earth in around the fence posts. They grabbed the hand of Christian and hung onto it.

"We thought the fish had you, Mr. Christian," said the girl.

Christian smiled at her. "They'll get me later on—for dessert, maybe," he said. Then to Townsend: "You always had good horses in the old days. I need half a dozen of the best. Can I buy them from you?"

"Having good horses is a habit that a gent don't wear out none too quick," said Townsend. "Sally, go round up the hosses and run 'em into the corral yonder. Come inside, gents, and we'll have a drink. I got some corn liquor that's worth while."

Townsend was a big man with a big, red face, and and a sun-faded growth of red hair on it. The hair was pale at the tip of the beard, and shining crimson near the skin from which it sprouted. He had a hearty manner and a smile unaffected, frank, open, and bold. He looked,

92

in spite of his ragged beard, like a boy grown bigger than his years. The wrinkles around his eyes seemed to come from too much smiling and laughter, not from time.

He took them into the house—it was a little three-room shack—and Bill Naylor admired out loud the neatness of the rooms.

"That's Sally," said Townsend. "She's the sort of a girl that doesn't have to idle around all day to cook three meals. Every lick counts when Sally puts it in. She's that sort of a girl. When she cooks, what she turns out is worth eating. When she talks, what she says is worth hearing."

Then he added: "Fetch up chairs. Sit around and make yourselves comfortable, partners. Christian, it's a great sight to me—seein' this here face of yours. I'd been thinkin' that Jim Silver had put you down at last."

He brought out a jug of whisky. It was almost colorless. There was only a faint taint of yellow in it, but it tasted fairly mellow.

"Sally made the whisky, too," said Townsend. "Her uncle had a still back in the hills a few years ago, and Sally learned how to run it. She made this stuff twelve years ago, believe it or not. And that was when she was ten years old. She was born with a brain and a pair of hands!"

He set out a jam made of wild blackberries—Sally had made it—and some cold pone, and fresh butter that was rather white—"because there ain't much green grass now, and Sally won't use no artificial colorin' stuff in the churn." They washed down the mouthfuls with generous swigs of the moonshine.

"What'll you do when Sally up and leaves you and marries?" asked Christian of the father.

"The man that marries her is a man that can lick me," said Townsend, grinning, "and the gent that can lick me is the right kind of a husband for her. Come on out, boys. She's got the hosses into the corral. Dog-gone me if she can't whistle 'em into that corral in five

93

minutes, where it always takes me half a day to run down the ornery broncs."

He led the way out to the corral, where a fine twisting, racing, bounding crowd of mustangs, perhaps thirty in all, were flashing through the dust of their own raising. The girl had just dismounted from a tall brown gelding to run into place the last bar of the corral gate. She came around the fence toward the house; the tall gelding followed her, hunting at the pockets of her overalls as if for sugar or apples.

Barry Christian stood right up on top of a fence post and stared down through the dust clouds and named the horses that he wanted. Townsend and Naylor went in and roped the selected animals. They were the pick of the lot. They might not be the prettiest, but they were the best. Naylor knew it, and he smiled to himself in admiration of his chief. Townsend said openly, when the five were tied outside the corral:

"I hoped you wouldn't pick out that gray. He's a mean-looking, ugly devil, and I hoped that you wouldn't look at his legs and shoulders too hard. You've got the cream of the lot, Barry! That's five of 'em. Did you say that you want six?"

"I want six," said Christian. "But I don't need any more of that lot. How about the brown gelding?"

"He's not for sale," said the girl. "Doc belongs to me. He's not for sale."

She had hoisted herself onto the top rail of the fence and sat there with one foot swinging. She wore narrow-toed boots like any cowpuncher, except that Bill Naylor had never seen a foot so small.

"I'll bargain with you," said Christian. "I'll give you two hundred and fifty. Three hundred, we'll call it."

"He's not for sale," said the girl.

"Five hundred flat," said Christian, folding his arms as he stood magnificently on the top of the post.

Bill Naylor looked up at him with a heightened admiration. Five hundred was a frightful price even

94

for a horse that looked as sound and as fast as the gelding.

"Not for sale," said the girl.

Her foot had stopped swinging. She sat up straight and defied her father with her eye. Naylor forgot his admiration of his chief in order to look at the girl more closely. She was no beauty. Beauties don't have freckles, and their noses are straight. But there was something about her that fitted his idea of what a woman should be as closely as the butt of a Colt fitted the grip of his hand.

"Not for sale at five hundred?" asked Christian.

"Wait a minute," broke in Townsend. "Don't be such a fool, Sally. Sure, Doc is for sale at five hundred."

"He's not," said the girl. "He belongs to me, and he's not for sale."

"He belongs to me, if I want him," said Townsend angrily. "And he's sold if Christian offers five hundred. You can have the cash, but I want to teach you not to be a fool about a horse. A girl that'll be a fool about a horse will be ten times a fool about a man. I want you to keep your head in the pinches. Five hundred? It's too much! Sure, you can have the gelding, Barry!"

"Try him, Naylor," said Christian.

Naylor looked at the girl. The girl looked back at Naylor, and her face was a pale stone, hard set. Her eyes were glinting. She said not a word.

Naylor took the colt, lengthened the stirrups of the girl's saddle, and swung up. The colt that had gone smooth as silk for Sally Townsend now developed plenty of kinks and pitched like a savage. But by that bucking, Naylor knew that the gelding was sound as a drum and made of steel wire and springing whalebone. He rode the colt until it was in hand and then came and dismounted.

Christian stood on the ground now, at the side of Townsend, saying:

"That's a good one, eh, Bill?"

Naylor ran his thumb and forefinger through the

95

sweat and gloss of the shoulder of the horse. He shook his head.

"Weak in the legs, Barry," he answered. "Sort of horse that would let you down in a long day's work, I guess."

"Hey!" cried Townsend. "What is the——"

He checked himself, for Christian was saying: "All right. We'll get along with only five horses. That'll be enough till we get to the next place."

He gave a thick wad of money to Townsend who took it without counting and thrust it into his pocket. Townsend said to Naylor:

"I dunno where you learned to judge hosses, kid."

Naylor answered sharply: "I learned in a neck of the woods where every man has a right to his own opinion."

Townsend started a retort: "Hoss sense is better than the——"

"Hold on, Townsend," cautioned Christian. "I don't want any trouble between you and Naylor. Bill Naylor is one of my best men. You know, Townsend, you can't judge a bulldog by the shortness of his teeth!"

He laughed, and Townsend chuckled, also. Only the girl, as Naylor noted, did not smile.

While Naylor was getting the newly purchased horses together, Sally Townsend helped him, and she found a chance to say:

"Listen, Bill. Have you picked the right line?"

"What line?" he asked.

"Riding with Barry Christian," she answered.

He looked at her in great surprise.

"What d'you mean by that?" he demanded.

"Nothing to hurt your feelings," said the girl. "But you're not mean enough to win out in a gang like that. You have to be able to shoot around corners to live with Barry Christian's gang."

Nothing in his life had ever stunned him so much except one thing—the strange conduct of Jim Silver in loosing Duff Gregor. His brain was still buzzing with the speech of the girl when at last he mounted that

96

good gray with the ugly head and took the four other new horses on the lead.

Not mean enough?

All his life he had been "mean." Bigger and stronger boys, at school, had always avoided him because he was a "mean" fighter. When his back was to the wall, the rules had never counted with him. Now a slip of a girl told him that he was not "mean" enough to get on with the crew of Barry Christian!

Well, he had saved her horse to her, and she had understood that. Women are funny, anyway. You never can understand them.

He came out of his trance of reflection, as they rode away from the Townsend place, for Barry Christian was saying:

"I didn't want to doubt you, back there. I wouldn't do that—with strangers looking on. But the next time I want you to remember that nothing comes between you and your work, when you're with me. I don't care what women are to you when you're not on the job. But when you ride with me, nothing exists except the business on hand."

CHAPTER XVI

Outlaw Crew

THEY spent a week back in the hills, recruiting. By the end of that time, Christian's men were a dozen strong, and Barry Christian himself made No. 13.

"That's a lucky number for us," said Christian, "because we work by the opposites of most people!"

There was not a weak member of the crew. Pudge

97

Wayler was fat, to be sure, and he was the oldest of the lot, but there was not a man, outside of Christian, who was handier with a gun, or shot straighter once it was free from leather. Wayler and Pokey had shared in a jail break while they were serving a long sentence that had been imposed after they were gathered in the net by Jim Silver, up at Horseshoe Flat.

But every one of the others had done time, and plenty of it. Every one of them had worked with Christian in the past, and was prepared now to follow the great outlaw blindly. A harder lot, Bill Naylor had never seen. It was not easy for him to be afraid of other men, but of some of these fellows he was frankly in terror. If it came to a show-down, he knew that he would never take water; but there were fellows, like Pokey, who had no more humanity in them than a rattlesnake. They all accepted him and fraternized with him, because it was known that he had saved the life of the chief.

During the week, the chief event was the arrival of a big chestnut stallion which was assigned at once to Duff Gregor. Gregor was an excellent rider, but every one knew that the reason the horse was assigned to him was because, on an animal like this, he had played the rôle of Jim Silver in the town of Crow's Nest in that deal which had nearly put a million into the pockets of the outlaws. The fame of that deal was still ringing through the minds of men.

The horse was carefully dyed with an equipment of four black stockings, and his other marks were altered so as to conform to the celebrated pattern that appeared in Parade. Then Duff Gregor was made up to resemble Jim Silver. Two gray spots were made to appear in his hair above the temples, and a dozen little glinting scars were caused to glimmer on his face.

Naylor argued the point with his chief.

"Barry," he said, "I've seen Parade, and I've seen Jim Silver. Nobody that's ever looked the pair of 'em in the face would ever think that this couple did more than wear the wrong names."

Christian answered: "That's because you know there's a fraud. But people only see what they expect to see. Mind that! Besides, in the business we're following, no one ever wins without taking a mighty big chance!"

Naylor wrote down those words in his own memory. That same day he had something new to think about.

They had drifted down through the hills until they were fairly close to the town of Elsinore. The robbery was to take place the next day.

The Overland, on whose route the town of Elsinore was no more than a flag station, came winding up toward the place through a narrow valley that had been cut out by a frothing, shouting creek. In that valley they were to stop the train and take their chance at getting to the safe which held the cash. The plans were all laid in detail.

They had camped for the evening in a dense pine wood where they could venture on building a fire and having a hot meal.

The dynamite had been cooked down, and the soup that was drawn off had been confided to the care of a yegg named Steve Cassidy. The rest of the men were gathered around the fire, except for two outposts, who walked on guard. And while the talk went quietly around, and Barry Christian worked sedulously on the drawing of a map of the surrounding country, there was a sudden outbreak of noise from the direction of one of the outposts.

The noise brought all the men to their feet. Naylor noticed that they gave only one glance toward Christian; after that, each was ready to stand on his own defense, and form his own plans. In truth, they were a hand-picked lot.

Then, running through the trees toward them, came the voice of Pokey.

He was calling: "Barry! Barry! Hell has broke loose!"

He came panting and gasping into the firelight. His white, sweating face was wild with fear and excitement. He was making gestures with both hands, as usual.

99

"Barry, there's hell popping!" he cried, and ran up to his chief.

Christian changed a little in face and color, also. He said:

"There's only one thing in the world that can make you act up like this, Pokey. It's Jim Silver!"

The name struck cold chills down the back of Naylor. He saw the other men start, and he heard the quick, deep intake of their breath.

The name of Silver was lightning in every mind, it was plain.

Then Pokey was gasping out: "Yes! Jim Silver! It's Jim Silver!"

"Where?" said Christian. "Get yourself together, you fool! Did you let him trail you out of Elsinore? I should have had more sense than to let you go into that town. Where is he now? On your trail?"

"No, he's back there—back there in Elsinore!" said Pokey.

The courage of Pokey seemed to return, with his breath. It seemed to Naylor a wonderful thing that a mere glimpse of a man who remained now many miles away should maintain such terror in the heart of another. But that man was Jim Silver; Pokey had clashed with him once before, and those who had battled with Jim Silver once had sufficient cause to remember him forever.

Pokey, as he recovered his breath and his presence of mind, said: "It sort of hit me all in a heap. I turned around a corner, and there was Jim Silver! Right there in front of me!"

"And he saw you?" demanded Christian.

"There was a gang around him. There's always a gang around Silver. The fools that want to shake hands with him, and the crooks that want to 'borrow' money from him. They were thick around Silver. He was sort of wading through them, smiling a little, the way he does. I side-stepped into a shadow and did a quick fade-away. All the way back, I've been seeing the ghost

100

of him sliding along after me, not making any noise, stepping out easy and slow and silent, the way Silver does."

"You marched out of Elsinore the minute you found out that Silver was in town, eh?" demanded Christian, with a certain quiet and sinister meaning in his voice.

"No, not just that," sad Pokey. "I'm not such a fool as that. I went around to the hotel first, and found out that Silver was staying there. They've given him the best room in the hotel, looking over the main street, with three windows in it, and all of that!"

"Good work," said Christian. "Because so long as I know that, I can know one other thing—that Jim Silver will die in that room to-night."

Silence oppressed the others. With vaguely hopeful eyes that looked toward Christian, who was walking up and down beside the fire, the gang expected the plan of the action that was to wipe Jim Silver off the face of the earth.

Christian said: "You fellows expect something clever. But there's no need to be clever. We have an edge on all the rest of the people that ever measured themselves against Silver. Because Silver thinks that Barry Christian is dead, and the result is that he's stepping out big and bold. He's been in the habit of sleeping with only one eye open for years—since he first met me. But now he thinks that he can take it easy. Well, he'll find out that he's wrong!"

He stopped in his walking and looked over the crowd.

"What ones of you fellows will volunteer to go with me to-night and take a crack at Silver?" he asked.

There was a dead silence. Of all those hardy fellows, there was not a single one who would willingly put himself in the peril of Silver. Not one, for the sake of praise and rewards from Christian, would volunteer to ride on that service.

Christian said slowly, but without contempt in his voice: "You understand what I've just been saying—that the game is practically in our hands, that Silver doesn't

101

expect danger of this kind, and that therefore we'll be striking him doubly from the dark? Think it over, boys, and volunteer if you want to."

Naylor felt a strange tug at his heartstrings; it was like the impulse a man feels to throw himself from a height.

Then Pudge Wayler was saying: "Well, a fellow can only die once. I've stood in front of Silver in the old days, and I reckon that I can stand there again. I'll ride with you, if you want me, Barry."

"You're the best man that I could have along," answered Christian. "You have a pair of hands, and you have a head. One more is all that I'll ask for."

Pokey broke out: "You think I'm scared to death. And I am. Anybody with sense is scared after he's nearly rubbed shoulders with that man-eater and got off alive. But I'll go back there with you, Barry. I may be shaking inside, but my hand won't shake any, you can bet."

Christian said: "I'd as soon have you and Pudge as any two men in the world. There's no hurry. Pick out three good horses. We have plenty of time to get to Silver's hotel room before he gets there to go to bed. He'll die like Billy the Kid—in the dark."

CHAPTER XVII

Naylor's Plan

AN ODD, shaking nervousness possessed Bill Naylor. It was a thing that made time seem to rush past him as it speeds by a man condemned to death. It sent him quivering away to the place where the horses were picketed. It made him pick out the long-bodied, ugly-headed gray horse which Townsend had said was the pick of his mustangs. Bill Naylor had a saddle on the back of that horse before he realized with a clear brain that the imp of the perverse was driving him to do a deed of folly.

However, the impulse was a thing which he could by no means resist. He found himself in the saddle, and working the horse gradually away among the trees. Behind him, the voices of his companions in crime soon faded out. They would not be coming this way too quickly. Christian had said that there was plenty of time. But there was not plenty of time for Bill Naylor.

As soon as he was at a distance which would cover the beating of the hoofs of his horse from the ears of those wild wolves back there at the camp, Naylor put the mustang to a lope. The trees swayed steadily past him. They climbed the hill. They dropped into the shallow of the valley. There was no moon, and Naylor was glad of that. For he felt that by even the light of a candle he would be able to examine his heart and his mind and see that he was making an utter fool of himself. Yet he would not for anything give up the plan that he had already conceived.

He climbed the next hill. Off to his left the railroad tracks ran with a dull glimmering, like two narrow ribbons of water, toward the lights of the town, a handful of trembling yellow rays. Those lights spread out gradually and separated, and grew individually brighter as he approached. Still the mustang kept up that steady lope, half trot and half gallop, the lazy swing of the hind legs seeming to trundle the forequarters effortlessly over the ground. Bill Townsend had been right when he called this horse one of the best.

As Naylor came out of the sweet air of pines, the wind was blowing toward him from the town the acrid scent of wood smoke. It smelled to him like danger, the hot iron of danger. But he went on.

When he came to the edge of the town, he took lanes and alleys in order to work his way to the center of things. He tied the gray in front of the first saloon he

103

encountered after turning into the main street. Into the saloon itself he sauntered, laid money on the bar, and asked for a drink. There was not another patron in the place.

"What's the matter?" asked Naylor of the barkeeper. "This town going dry?"

The bartender was a sour little man with a twisted face. He walked the bottle of whisky down the varnished bar and halted it in front of Naylor.

"There's a lot of half-wits in this town," he said, "that would rather talk than drink, when anything happens. And with a gent like Silver in town, they'd rather stand around and shift their weight from one leg to another than stand at a bar and make themselves comfortable."

"Well, Silver's quite a man," suggested Naylor.

"Yeah. He's a man. But whisky's always whisky," said the barkeeper.

"True," said Naylor. "Lemme have another. Where's Silver now?"

The bartender laughed, his face twisting more than ever.

"Where none of these gents can see him," said he. "Silver's back in the rear room of Tod Wilson's place with the door locked, drinking beer with Taxi. Nacherally, he don't want no strangers around when he's drinking with Taxi, does he? But Tod's barroom is packed—just because they all aim to get a look at Silver when he comes out from talking with Taxi, I suppose."

Naylor finished drinking his second whisky, which he had poured very small, and went to Tod Wilson's place. It was not hard to find. The movements of the men in the street were all toward that saloon, and the sidewalk was filled with people who slowly oozed into the place, and slowly trickled out again.

For half a minute, Naylor stood still and considered the throng. That was what it meant to be an honest man. Others were willing to give up their minds, their time, their money for a mere glimpse of such a fellow as Jim Silver. But Silver had paid for this attention with blood.

104

He would pay more blood, before very long. He might very well pay for it with his death before morning.

Naylor made no effort to get through the front door. Instead, he went down the side of the low shack, climbed a high board fence, and dropped into the back yard. All the rear end of the house was in darkness, except for one eye of light that leaked out at the corner of a shutter.

Naylor put his eye to that peek hole and found himself looking into a small room that had foot-worn linoleum on the floor, two or three small tables, and chairs around them. At one of the tables sat the Great Jim Silver, tilting a little back in his chair. Opposite him was a much smaller man, more slenderly made, with a dark and almost handsome face. The fringe of the long eyelashes made a distinct streak on his face, like a dark pencil marking. And he rarely looked up from his task.

That task was unique enough almost to identify him. For he had in front of him a small lock of polished steel, and as he worked over it, probing with a sliver of steel at the interior of the lock, sometimes he lowered his head and appeared to listen to the delicacy of the work which he was carrying on inside the lock.

That was Taxi, of course, the lock master, who could walk through the most complicated bolts and bars as if he possessed a magic gift. And now, as he sat opposite his best friend—who could tell how long they had been separated, and how many strange adventures had befallen each of them since the last meeting?—Taxi kept his attention riveted on the lock before him, and appeared to give very little heed to the words of famous Jim Silver.

Then, though there had not been a single sound, the head of Taxi turned with flashing speed, and he stared at the very shutter through which Naylor was peering. It was a startling thing to see those eyes, strangely pale and bright beneath the obscuring shadow of the lashes. It was like something in a dream, and a bad dream, at that.

That single, dangerous glance was all that Taxi gave toward the window. Then he returned his attention to

105

his lock. One could not tell whether he were nodding and faintly smiling because of the pleasure he took in his task, or whether it was because of what the soft, grave voice of Jim Silver was saying.

It seemed to Naylor, as he looked in on those two celebrated fellows, that the difference between them was like the difference between panther and lion.

Naylor went to the rear of the house, found a door, discovered that it was unlocked, and pulled it open. He stepped straight into the room where Silver and Taxi had been seated. They were seated no longer. They were both standing, looking curiously toward the opening of the door.

There was no more chance of surprising that pair than of surprising a couple of wild cats, lean with hunger, in the winter of the year.

Naylor came slowly in toward them.

"The man who set Gregor free," he heard the quiet voice of Silver say. "Taxi, meet Mr. Naylor."

Taxi looked at Naylor with a curling lip. He seemed ready to spring at the newcomer's throat. But he took Naylor's hand and merely muttered:

"Jim, I can't follow your ideas, half the time."

"I want to see you," said Naylor to Silver.

"Do you want to see me alone?" asked Silver.

"Yes, alone."

"Outside?"

"That's the best place," said Naylor.

"All right," said Silver.

He started toward the door, but Taxi exclaimed:

"Jim, what are you thinking about? Step out there into the dark with him? You might as well step into the mouth of a tiger!"

Silver lifted his hand with a faint smile.

"There are always chances, Taxi," he said, "but I'll bet on this one."

Christian had said something like that, as Naylor could remember. Was there, after all, some kind of a peculiar affinity between the two great enemies?

106

Then Naylor found himself outside the house and standing in the dimness of the starlight beside Silver. He knew, as he stood there, that no matter what might come out of the future, he had been right in making the ride.

"Silver," he said, "you did me a good turn, and I want to do you another."

"Thanks," said Silver. "What is it?"

"I want to ask you not to go back to your room in the hotel, to-night."

"I'm not to go back to the room in the hotel," echoed Silver quietly. "And why not?"

"Because there might be trouble waiting for you."

"Ah? How soon will the trouble be there?"

"I'm asking you," said Naylor, "not to go back to your room. If you fish around to find trouble—well, you may find it, all right, but you'll land me in the soup. I'm asking you to take my word for it and let the thing go. Will you do that?"

Silver was silent. In the darkness, he looked bigger than ever, to Naylor. He looked so big a target that a child could hardly fail to hit him, even in the obscurity of an unlighted room. Starlight was enough for the shooting of a prize of this rating.

Suppose that he, Bill Naylor, pulled a gun and tried a point-blank shot for the heart—well, he would be famous forever. It hardly mattered how a man like Jim Silver was killed. To be his slayer was to go down in history. And, in the old days, Naylor felt that the opportunity would have been a sad temptation.

But he found himself saying to the big, silent man: "I can't talk names to you. All I can do is to give you some advice—and ask you not to pull me into the soup."

Silver said, at last: "All right. I had an idea when I left you before, that there'd be something good coming out of you, Naylor. I'm thanking you now just as though I could look inside my room in the hotel and see the men and the guns waiting for me. But"—here he sighed—"you don't want me to trap 'em?"

107

"No," said Naylor. "I'd be a—a traitor, if you did."

"I don't want you to be that," answered Silver. "Come in and have a drink with me."

"I'm overdue in another place," said Naylor. "I was overdue the second that I left it."

"And your neck's in danger now?" said Silver. "You're in trouble on account of me?"

"I'm not in trouble on account of you," said Naylor suddenly, the words taking command of him. "I'm in trouble because I've been a crook and a thug all the days of my life."

He gripped the hand of Jim Silver with a sudden gesture and then hurried away into the darkness.

CHAPTER XVIII

Sally's Decision

IN SPITE of Naylor's hurry, in spite of the fact that there might be literal danger to his neck if he were missed during this long absence, he did not aim straight back at the camp, but swung a little to the south of the straight line and came out through the hills in sight of the Townsend ranch.

There was a moon, by this time. It stood in the east like a pale ship of an ancient design, and the light from it blanched the hills and painted long black shadows beside them.

Naylor rode down to the rear of the hay shed and there tethered the gray horse and pulled off its saddle After that, he went to the side of the little ranch house. He felt that it was a lucky break that had brought him into the house not many days before, so that now he

108

knew in which room the girl slept. Standing at the low window, he tapped lightly on the sill.

When he had no answer, he leaned a little across the sill and listened. He could hear regular breathing, and there was a faint delicacy of perfume in the air. That was strange, he thought. She was not the sort of a girl to use perfume. But one never can tell about women. It is best not to waste time trying to foretell their characters.

He hissed, and rapped the sill of the window again.

The regular noise of the breathing ended; there was a creaking of springs, and then:

"Who's there?"

"Be quiet," commanded Naylor. "No robber, Sally."

"Hi!" he heard her say, under her breath. "It's Bill Naylor!"

The moon slanted into the room and hit the foot of the bed. In the thick of the darkness beyond the moonlight, vaguely he saw the girl get out of the bed and throw a bath robe around her. She came toward him. Her bare, brown feet walked through the moonlight. The feet looked soft. The ankles were small and gave inward slightly. She walked like an Indian, toeing straight ahead. Her elbows were up as she swung her long hair into a knot behind her head. Then she sat down on the window sill.

It had not taken her five seconds, he thought, to get from the bed to the window.

"Hi, Bill," said she. "How's things?"

"So, so," said Naylor. He had taken off his hat, and now he grinned at her. He wished, suddenly, that he were inches taller. He almost wished that a face surgeon could work for a time on his face to make him more handsome. For now that he could not see the freckles across her nose, the girl looked beautiful to him. She was sun-browned like an Indian, but she was beautiful.

"Is this a dog-gone serenade, or something?" said the girl.

109

"Quit it, will you?" said Bill Naylor. "If I started caterwauling, you'd think that a wolf had come down out of the hills."

"D'you wanta see dad, then?" she asked. "He's a light sleeper, and the whisky jug isn't sealed."

"Thanks," said Naylor.. "You think that I'd ride all this way for the sake of a drink?"

"Go on, tell me why you came," urged the girl. "Say something nice, and tell me why you came, will you?"

She put her chin on her fist and looked at him.

"How deep are you laughing at me?" asked Naylor.

"Skin-deep," said the girl.

"Skin-deep, eh?"

"Yeah," she said. "That's as far as beauty goes."

She laughed, silently, shaking with her mirth.

"Quit it, will you?" said Naylor. "I'm no handsome bird. I know that."

"Just a good, dependable, home boy, eh?" she asked.

She kept on laughing. She was always laughing. There was a river of mirth pulsing in her throat like a song. Her teeth flashed in the moonlight.

He made a cigarette, lighted it, and blew out smoke. The smoke was as silver-pale as frosted fog, in the moonlight.

"I had to rush over here and tell you something," said Naylor.

"Rush on with it, then," said the girl, nodding.

He came up close to the window sill and took hold of her hand. There was nothing scary about her. She was as steady as a man. There was nothing silly or simpering about her, either. She looked him straight in the eyes.

"Listen," said he.

"Have you scalped somebody?" asked the girl. "What's the matter with you, being all nervous, like this?"

"I ain't nervous," argued he. "I'm just telling you something. What time is it?"

"That's not telling me anything. That's asking something."

"Quit kidding me. What time is it, about?"

110

"It struck one, a little while back."

"You went to bed when?"

"Ten thirty. Why?"

"Well," said he, "I wanta tell you something. You went to bed at ten thirty, and about eleven o'clock, just as you were getting your eyes shut——"

"You mean it takes me half an hour to go to sleep?" said Sally Townsend. "Don't be silly. At the end of a Townsend day on this man's ranch nobody needs to be sung to sleep. When my head hits the pillow, I'm out like a light. But what're you driving at?"

"Give me a chance to tell you, will you? At about eleven o'clock, just after you hit the hay, you heard a tapping at the window, and you sat up and saw me looking in. I'd come over here from the camp. Understand?"

"That's all right," said the girl. What did you come for?"

"I dunno. I just come over. You see? Don't forget it. And I stayed around here talking with you for a couple of hours. I've been here since eleven o'clock."

"Look here, Bill," said the girl, "what are you trying to put over on me?"

"I'm not putting nothing over. I'm asking you to do me a good turn, that is all."

"Then come clean, will you?"

"What do you mean, come clean?"

"Tell me all about it. You been out gadding?"

"I've been out," said Naylor. "That's all I can tell you."

"Who'll check you up for playing hookey?" said the girl.

"Somebody who's worse than the devil when he gets riled."

"You mean Barry Christian?"

"That's who I mean."

He sighed as he said it.

"Well," said the girl, "have you crossed up Barry in any way, to-night?"

111

"No matter what I've done," said he, "I'm asking you to do me a good turn."

"Does it sound as simple as all of that to you?"

"What's the matter? You just let people know—if they should happen to ask—that I arrived here at eleven and didn't leave till after one."

"That'll be fine for me!" said the girl grimly. "Look here, Bill. You're not that sort of a fellow. You don't want to get me into that sort of a jam, do you?"

"What's the matter?" asked Bill Naylor.

"Why, suppose you had a sister or a daughter, or something, and she got out of bed and talked to a man she'd only seen once before—talked to him for a couple of hours? What would you think? What would you do?"

"I see what you mean," said Bill Naylor slowly. "I didn't think about that. I'm just dumb, I guess. Forget about what I asked you to say; go back to bed and go to sleep, Sally."

"And what comes of you?"

"Oh, I'm all right. I'll get through, all right. There won't be any pinch."

"If there is, you'll be dead from it. I know Barry Christian as well as you do. Listen, Bill. What crazy thing have you done to Barry Christian?"

"I should be telling you, eh?" asked Naylor.

"You were telling me that you called on me at eleven and didn't leave till one."

A little thrill of desperation ran coldly through his nerves. He gave her hand a hard grip. He stuck out his jaw and looked her right in the face.

"I'll tell you what I did, beautiful," said he. "I'll tell you that Silver's in Elsinore; and Barry Christian knows he's there; and Christian and a couple more are lying in Silver's hotel room, right now, waiting for him to come in. But Silver won't come in. He won't—because I told him to stay away. I didn't tell him what was in his room. I told him to stay away from it."

"Did you actually do that?" whispered the girl. "Did you mix up between Christian and Jim Silver?"

112

"Yeah. I'm bright, I guess," said Bill Naylor. "I mixed in between them, and now I'll catch it. I don't know what's the matter with me," he added, in a faintly groaning complaint. "I never made a fool of myself like this before!"

"Look, Bill," said the girl, "maybe you're a better man than you ever thought. I told you that you were too soft to play around with Barry Christian and his gang."

"That was because you softened me up a little," argued Naylor. "I'm hard enough, beautiful. Don't let anybody tell you nothing different. I'm hard enough."

"Hard enough to do time, eh?"

"Yeah, plenty," said Bill Naylor. "Well, I gotta go and sashay back to the camp. So long, Sally."

"Wait a minute," said the girl.

"What for?"

"While I think. I gotta think something out."

"Go on and think, then," said Naylor. "You can think just as well while I'm on the road."

"No. I'm just thinking that maybe you *did* get here at eleven and stay till one. I don't care what people say."

"I do, though," said Naylor. "I was a tramp to ever ask you to say that. I didn't think."

"Quit it. I've got to think," she said.

She dropped her chin on her fist again. The moon painted her frown black. It made her face look old. Her nostrils quivered and expanded a little. Naylor saw how she would appear when she was ten years older. But he hardly cared. She would always look good to him.

"Well," she said, with a sigh, "people can go hang. You got here at eleven o'clock, all right."

"No, I didn't. I won't put that over on you."

"You can't help yourself. That's the story I tell. If you don't stick to it, you make a fool out of me and maybe you lose your scalp. Be yourself, Bill. Wake up and be yourself."

He looked at her for a long time, feature by feature.

"Sally," said Naylor, "you're not very old or very big, but you're great. You know that? You're great."

113

"We were talking about something for two hours," said the girl. She chuckled suddenly. "That was what we were talking about. You came over to tell me that I was great. It was something I didn't know and I wanted to hear about it. I heard about it for two hours, sitting right here on the window sill."

"Sure," said Naylor. "That's all right. We were talking about you. I'll tell you what, I came over here to tell you that I'm nutty about you, Sally."

"That's a good one, too," said Sally. She chuckled again. "Good old Bill," she said. "That's all right, too."

"Wait a minute," said Bill Naylor. "I *am* nutty about you. You're the goods. I'm crazy about you, Sally!"

"Good old Bill," she repeated. "What a lingo you've got. You're a regular snake charmer."

"Am I talking like a fool?" said Naylor. "Anyway, I mean what I say. I don't know how to make you believe me. I never talked to a girl like this."

"No?" said she.

"The females all back up and shy when they see my map," said Bill. "I never had a chance to work up any lingo, you know. It's my tough mug that stops 'em at a distance."

"It's a good enough mug," said the girl. "It ought to wear pretty well, Bill."

"I gotta be going," said Naylor.

"So long," said the girl. "If you get back quick and sneak in, maybe nobody'll spot you."

"That's right," said Naylor. "You think of things."

"Go on, then. Hurry it up, Bill."

He started to turn away, but could not move his feet.

"It's hard to go," said Naylor. "Because there's nobody like you. I feel pretty dog-gone queer, Sally."

"Where?" said she.

He put his arms around her. She sat up straight on the window sill and looked into his face.

"You'd better do some thinking," she said.

"I've done more thinking right here than I've done in all the rest of my life," said Bill Naylor.

114

"Have you?" said the girl.

She put her hand on his forehead and pushed her fingers back through the tough scrub of his hair, tilting back his head till the moon got at his face.

"You *are* a tough-looking mug," said the girl.

"Yeah, I'm something fierce to look at. If you're doing any thinking—I've been in for everything from smuggling to stick-up work. I ain't even been bright. Any dumb cop could pinch me. Only I'm crazy about you, Sally."

"Well," said the girl, "I've been doing some thinking, too."

"About what?" he asked.

"About the way you arrived at eleven, and you told me you were crazy about me, and I said I was crazy about you. That would take a couple of hours, all right."

"Hold on," said Naylor hoarsely. His whole body began to shudder. "You have to think it all out before you talk like that. This is for good and all."

"Sure it is," said Sally Townsend. "But I wish that you wouldn't go back to Barry Christian. Not if you know Jim Silver well enough to even brush his boots with your best hat!"

CHAPTER XIX

In the Morning

WHEN Bill Naylor got back to the camp, he used a very simple device for getting past the outer guard. He simply took saddle and bridle off the gray mustang and then walked beside it carrying the paraphernalia. On that side of the camp stalked the lengthy form of "Crane"

115

Bushwick. He stopped long enough to whistle softly to the mustang, and then to laugh as the horse came edging on, worked along by the nudging elbows of Naylor, who walked bent over on the farther side.

Crane Bushwick went on with his beat, humming softly to himself, paying no heed, for a number of the horses had been turned loose to graze beyond the trees which sheltered the camp. And as the gray mustang walked ahead, Naylor was presently in the safe sanctuary of the pines.

There, in a small clearing, he hobbled the gray as most of the other horses were hobbled, and he paused long enough to rub down the mustang with bunches of pine needles. For if there were an examination, he did not wish the horse to show the encrusted sweat that is always present after a long and hard ride.

Finally, there was the move to get to his blankets. He had made up his bunk on the outer rim of the firelighted circle, and now from the shelter of a big tree trunk he looked over the scene. The firelight, he was glad to see, had dwindled. The fire was almost out, and the embers stared with steady, red eyes. Only when a breeze worked in among the trees was there an upward flickering of the flame that set all the scene around wavering like a thing seen beneath rippling waves.

He made sure that all of the men were in their places. He found only three made-up blanket beds which were empty—those of the three men who had ridden to town to waylay Jim Silver.

Bill Naylor shook his head when he thought of how he had forestalled them! His whole code of faith was much perturbed by the thing he had done. To Bill Naylor it had always been proper to serve one's own ends in most affairs, but when occupied in any sort of work, one must serve one's comrades as oneself. In this case, he had deliberately thwarted his great man, his Barry Christian, by carrying the warning to Jim Silver.

Naylor could not tell what to think of his own conduct. There was one solitary consolation, and this was

116

that of the girl, Sally Townsend, had seemed to approve. She was, to be sure, only a woman; but she was certainly unlike all others of her sex.

Even about Sally his feelings were mixed. Suppose that his old comrades of many illegal adventures were to hear that he had married, what would they say? What was he himself to say of the thought? Was he fit to marry a decent person? What sort of a future could he offer to her?

He thought of those things as he stood behind the pine tree, looking over the camp. Finally he muttered to himself: "You're bein' a fool, Bill Naylor!"

This quiet comment from his own lips set him in motion toward his blankets. He had reached them unobserved, he was certain when the flame of the fire reached a resinous knot in a bit of firewood and made it explode with a loud, snapping noise.

Some one grunted, and as Naylor sank down on his blankets, he saw a figure sitting bolt upright on the far side of the fire. It was Steve Cassidy, yegg extraordinary. And as he said nothing, but simply stared, Naylor was assured that the safe blower had ugly thoughts in his mind.

He wished, as he fell asleep, that any man in the camp, other than Steve Cassidy, had seen him.

Once before morning, Naylor wakened, and was aware of a hushed bustling around him. Three men had just returned. He opened one eye and observed them.

He saw the tall, gaunt form of Pokey and heard him mutter: Rottenest luck I ever heard of!"

Well, that was one thing finished. It was apparent that they had returned without doing any harm to Jim Silver, and it was also apparent that Jim Silver had not taken advantage of the information he had received in order to do harm to them.

About this second point Bill Naylor did a good deal of thinking, as he lay awake for a moment and stared up past the narrow points of the evergreens into the blue-black of the sky. He could see a swarm of little

117

stars, a cloud of them, and in addition there was one big bluish point of fire. Was it a planet or was it a star of the first magnitude? He could not tell, but he had a feeling that that was the way Jim Silver shone among other men, no matter how bright the rest might be.

On that thought he went to sleep again and when he roused the next morning, he discovered that every one else was already astir. The gray of the dawn had ended and the golden time had begun. And beside him stood Pudge Wayler, in the very act of poking him in the ribs again with the toe of a boot.

The indignity enraged Bill Naylor and got him to his knees in a flash.

He was ready to hit Wayler when the sour, rumbling voice of the other man said:

"If you wanta fight, save it for the chief. He wants to talk to you, brother."

Well, the fight went suddenly out of Naylor, at that. He got into his boots, washed his face and hands and shaved at the nearest run of water, and then went to where fragrant steam was rising from the big pot where coffee was being made. Barry Christian already was poising a tin cup on his knee. He looked up calmly at Naylor as the latter came to him. And suddenly Naylor found an exact parallel for the color and the brightness of those eyes; for he could remember how Taxi had looked toward the shuttered window the night before.

The outlaw chief said, simply: "You got in pretty late, last night. Where were you?"

"Oh, no place," said Naylor.

It was the speech of a fool, and he felt like a fool after he had uttered it.

"Think it over," said Christian. "You were somewhere, I guess. You got in late. Cassidy saw you get in at pretty near two o'clock this morning. Where were you?"

Cassidy was a fellow with a crumpled, broken face. He had a broken jaw and a broken nose. His blond hair was always rumpled. His brow was constantly disturbed by a troubled frown. Now he looked wearily toward

118

Naylor, and up and down Naylor's body. It was plain that he did not care about any man's displeasure. Certainly he was not concerned as to whether or not Naylor disapproved of him.

Bill Naylor said: "I don't want to make a fool of myself. I'll tell you the first time we're alone, chief. I'll tell you where I was."

Barry Christian looked right through him.

"You might as well speak out now. You know that I went in with Pudge and Pokey last night, to wait for Jim Silver in his room. We found the room, all right. We waited there all night. But Jim Silver never showed up! It looked as though somebody had warned him that there might be trouble in that room last night. Well, no one could have warned him from this camp. Everybody was accounted for—except you! And you got in about two o'clock. Where were you?"

"Yeah," said Pokey, under his breath, "where were you?"

"You mean," said Naylor, repeating the idea as though in loathing of it, "you mean that I might have sneaked in ahead and warned Jim Silver, might 'a' told him that you were going to wait for him in his room?"

"That's what I mean. You're not a fool, Bill," said Christian. "That's what I mean, all right. Now tell me where you were!"

"Why," said Naylor, "did Silver jump you and try to bag you? You mean to say that the three of you got through a trap that Silver set for you, and none of you hurt?"

"He means," explained Pudge Wayler, speaking to himself, "that if Silver had had word, he wouldn't 'a' let it go with just staying away from the room. He would 'a' tried to bag us. I dunno. I didn't think of that."

Christian suddenly stood up and dashed his coffee cup to the ground. His voice, usually so persuasive and soft, rang thundering against the frightened ears of the guilty man.

"Answer me! Where were you, Naylor?"

119

"Chief," said Naylor, "I was only over seeing a girl. That was all."

"A girl? A girl?" exclaimed Barry Christian. "What girl? I was afraid—and now I'm practically sure! Naylor, if you've come between me and Jim Silver, no matter what you've done for me, no matter if you're more than a brother to me, I'll have the best blood out of your heart—and I'll have it now! What girl are you talking about?"

"Why, Barry," said Naylor, "I mean the Townsend girl. That's all I mean. I went over to talk to her last night. I thought that it might be the last chance."

"Maybe it is—maybe it was!" said Christian savagely.

He stared at Naylor, and his eyes were more like the eyes of Taxi than ever—balls of pale fire. His whole face grew pale. It seemed to Naylor as luminous as steel.

"Pokey—Cassidy—take the guns off Naylor, and cart him over to the Townsend place. Get the facts out of the Townsend girl. If you think that Naylor has lied—shoot him dead, and come back here. Lay him dead right across the threshold of the Townsend ranch house. It'll teach some of these ranchers what it means to double-cross Barry Christian."

That was the way they went about it.

Yonder in the town of Elsinore was Jim Silver, who had kept faith and declined to bag scoundrels who were lying in wait for him in the darkness of his own room. Jim Silver had kept faith perfectly. But here with Barry Christian it was a different matter.

Then another thought occured to Bill Naylor. He told himself that no man could lead as Christian led unless he had a soul as hard as chilled steel. No man could go on to so many triumphs unless he had the cruelly stern nature of Christian. If one man failed Christian and the gang, that man had to go to the wall were he Christian's own brother!

Naylor was frightened, but he could not say that even in this moment of supreme trial he really hated Christian. He was too big and important for such emotions. It

120

would be like hating a tiger to hate Christian. It was as easy to expect mercy and tenderness from a wild beast.

Naylor saw this, at last. He thought of the way he had pulled the man from the water of Kendal River. He thought of the way he had nursed him, of the dangerous expedition he had made to the town of Blue Water for the sake of Barry Christian, of the manner in which, for the sake of Christian, he had saved Duff Gregor from the men of Crow's Nest. But all of these services would be forgotten if, for an instant, he had come between Christian and the hatred which the great outlaw felt for Jim Silver.

Well, the thing was almost justified. The hate of Christian for Silver had made history in the past and it would make history in the future.

He pondered these things as he was "fanned" for his guns. Then he was taken between Cassidy and Pokey to the Townsend ranch.

Cassidy said, when the gray mustang was saddled: "If he rode all the way to Elsinore, last night, he wasn't on this mustang. There ain't enough sweat marks on it. Besides, it's still full of ginger!"

That was true, also, for the inexhaustible meanness of the gray mustang induced it to try to pitch off its rider as soon as Naylor got into the saddle. He blessed the fierce nature of the gray at that moment!

They got to the ranch to find that Bill Townsend and his daughter were busily stringing wire on the fence posts of the new corral. Townsend worked the lever which stretched the wire while his daughter in a workmanlike manner whacked home the big brads that fastened the wire to the posts. They stopped work to watch the approach of the trio.

It was Cassidy who spoke first. He touched his hat to the girl and said:

"Hello, Townsend. Come over here from the chief. He wants to know if this gent here, this fellow Naylor,

121

was really over here chinning with your girl, last night from around eleven to one?"

"Him?" said Townsend. "He sure wasn't. If he was, I'd knock his block off. A runt like that make eyes at Sally? I'd tear him in two!"

The girl said nothing.

"You hear that?" said Cassidy grimly, to Naylor.

There was no mistaking Cassidy. He was the type to put cold lead in any man, with or without orders. Yes, and to enjoy the doing of it, too!

"I hear," said Naylor. "There's a lot that Townsend doesn't know, maybe. That's all I can say."

"Is that all?" said Pokey savagely.

"Wait a minute," urged Cassidy.

He turned to the girl.

"What about this yarn of Naylor coming over here to talk to you for a couple of hours last night?"

"What business is it of yours?" asked the girl angrily.

Naylor, with a vast relief of spirit, saw that she intended to be as good as her word, and lie in his behalf.

"I gotta make it my business," said Cassidy. "Let's have an answer—if you care enough to get up and talk to this gent for two hours by night, you can say two words for him by day."

"Well, he was here, and what of it?" said the girl.

Pokey grunted as though it were bad news to him. Cassidy turned his deformed face and stared at Naylor.

"All right, old son," he said. "I guess that lets you out."

"Wait a minute!" shouted Townsend. "Lets him out? It don't let him out at all. You mean to say, Naylor, you worthless hound, that you were over here last night talking to my girl? Sally, is that right?"

She said nothing. Townsend charged like a bull, but Naylor spun the gray mustang about and fairly fled from the danger. At that, the big hand of Townsend clutched for him and barely missed his coat sleeve.

In the near distance, Naylor pulled up again, and saw Townsend gesticulating behind him.

But the two of the escort were laughing as they came up.

"That saves your hide, Naylor," said Pokey, as he ranged his horse alongside. "You wouldn't blame Christian for being heated up if he thought that you had crossed him with Silver, would you?"

They got back to the camp, and Christian heard the report. He nodded. There was no apology for the suspicion he had fixed upon Naylor. He simply said:

"Then if Naylor didn't carry word, somebody else did. Watch yourselves, boys, because we have a traitor with us. And when we catch him, he'll wish that he'd got to hell in any way except through our hands. However, this is a busy day, and the crook will have to wait for to-morrow."

That was the point at which Bill Naylor made up his mind that he was through with Barry Christian and all his men.

CHAPTER XX

A Stroke of Bad Luck

THE plan for the train robbery was perfectly simple. Down the valley, several miles below Elsinore, the railroad track made a quick bend, and at a point where the engineer of the speeding train would not see the obstruction until the last available moment, Christian had several trees felled right across the rails. There would be just comfortable time, as he figured it, for the engineer to clap on the brakes and bring the train to a halt after the locomotive rounded the bend into view of the obstacle.

The place was ideally equipped in every way. For on either side of the way there was plenty of tall brush where a thousand men could have hidden, and there were several clumps of trees, in two of which the horses were tied.

Christian had drilled his men carefully in the details of the work. Certain ones were to master the engineer and fireman, force them to flood the firebox—so that the train could not proceed on its way for help too quickly after the robbery had come to an end.

Others—and this was the most important detail, of course—were to make the attack on the mail car, where the safe was located that should contain the big shipment of cash. And four men were detailed to take charge of the passengers and keep them in the coaches until the fighting was finished. Afterward, the passengers could be paraded outside the cars and searched for valuables.

The plan was simple, but of course there was plenty of danger attached to it. For one thing, the guards in the treasure car were likely to put up a savage fight that might delay the procedure for hours, even. And then in the body of the passenger coaches there might be a number of armed men ready to battle for their rights. Every Westerner in the train was reasonably sure to have a weapon, and to be able to use it. The force of surprise would be half the battle to decide the issue in favor of the gang.

Every man was in his place at least an hour before the time the train was due. That hour was the most trying of all. For as Bill Naylor crouched in the shade of a bush, shifting here and there as patches of the yellow sunshine began to burn through the thickness of his coat like boiling liquid, he thought of a number of things that could happen. There was the danger, for instance, that the warning might have been given, and that when the train arrived, it would consist of coaches filled with keen riflemen who would pour out, sweep through the brush, and gather in every last man of the robbers. That had happened before in the history of the breaking of law in the West. It was not a pleasant prospect.

There were other troubles to have in mind. And a good big .45-caliber slug would put a man on the ground in such shape that Christian, no matter how solicitous for the welfare of his men, could not take the wounded away with him.

Well, if a fellow were snagged in that manner, it might mean anything from fifteen years to hanging, according as to whether or not any one on the train were killed.

But something more than his own personal danger began to trouble the brain of Bill Naylor. The girl had wished one Jim Silver for him to follow rather than a thousand like Barry Christian. And though it was true that her father kept moonshine liquor and sold horses to robbers, something told Naylor that the girl was a different cut from her father. She had to submit to life as she found it; but when she started off for herself, there was something straight and clean about her eyes that told Naylor she would fight with all her might on the side of honesty and the law.

He looked gloomily around him. Of course, it was far too late to withdraw, not only because withdrawal would brand him as a coward, but also because it was known that Chirstian never allowed a man to leave the ranks when trouble was on hand. Once a follower of Barry Christian, always a follower. That was the law of the band. And it seemed to Naylor that he was thinking of another man in another era when he remembered the awe and delight with which he had at first looked forward to being one of Christian's trusted men.

Off to the side, Pokey and Cassidy were shaking dice, not for money they had in pocket, but for money they expected to have before this day was ended.

Duff Gregor came strolling by slowly. Duff always moved slowly, as though he wanted people to mark him with care. Most of the men in the gang had little use for him, but every one treated him with a certain amount of respectful consideration because of the fact that he

125

had once played the rôle of the great Jim Silver, and because he was made up to play the same rôle again. Just what advantage could be gained from that part now it was hard to say. But Christian undoubtedly had something important in mind. He was not the fellow to waste moves.

Bill Naylor had had a chance to talk to a number of the men and find out from them their exact feelings about Silver. It seemed that they all regarded him with a queer mixture of terror and loathing and wonder. The terror and wonder were explicable, and the loathing came, it appeared, from their feeling that it was unnatural for a man to fight on the side of the law unless the law had given him a place, a title, and a respectable salary. Amateur bloodhounds were considered savage freaks of nature.

"Suppose," men said, "that everybody took the same angle that Jim Silver does, what sort of a chance would the rest of us have, eh?"

There was enough in this remark to make Bill Naylor want to smile a little. But he realized, also, that as little as a month before he would not have smiled at all!

Naylor was in the midst of these reflections when the first stroke of bad luck hit the men of Christian and their plans. On the top of the hills to the right of the track appeared the figure of a boy on horseback, without a saddle, heading his mustang after a long-legged steer that had, apparently, broken loose from the bunch the boy was riding herd on. The youngster was on the very verge of cutting off the steer in its flight and sending it back when the foolish animal made a sudden turn and bolted right down the steep slope toward the railroad.

The slope was so sharp that the steer, once well under way, had to brace itself on all four legs. It bellowed with fear and catapulted to the bottom of the grade. There it rolled head over heels, but Western steers are made of whalebone and leather, and therefore the neck of this beef was not broken. It recovered its feet, shook its head

126

to clear its addled brains, and bolted again into the brush which sheltered half of the gang of Barry Christian.

That would hardly have mattered, but the second half of the little drama was what mattered. For the boy, after angling for one moment on the verge of the slope, suddenly whipped his mustang right down in pursuit of the steer. Considering the shortness of the brown, bare legs that gripped the barrel of the horse, and the absence of any stirrups, it was as bold a bit of horsemanship as Bill Naylor had ever seen. He saw the boy's face puckered and his eyes staring with fear, but down he came, with a ringing whoop to raise his own spirits.

In the meantime the steer, as the boy and the mustang safely caromed to the foot of the slope, had flung up its tail and fled, bawling. It seemed so blinded by fear that it had not sufficient sense to dodge the brush, but went crashing straight through a big bush behind which Pokey and Cassidy were playing their game of dice. Pokey leaped up to one side, with a yell. Cassidy, knocked sprawling, rose up on the other. Two or three other men sprang up from the brush as the course of the steer suddenly threatened them.

That was sufficient to turn the steer; but it was also sufficient to tell the boy that a whole band of armed men was hiding out in the shrubbery. That was enough for him. He turned the head of his pony away from the steer and fled on a straight line for the nearest trees— and toward Elsinore, far away!

Every one realized the importance of the episode. No youngster able to ride like that and take such chances could fail to realize that those armed men had not gathered together merely to sit in the shade and waste their time. He would probably go right on to Elsinore as fast as his swift little mustang could carry him.

"Stop him!" shouted the great voice of Christian as he rose. "Shoot the horse from under him!"

Shoot the horse from under him? Who in the world could determine his shooting so exactly as to be sure of

127

striking the horse, and not the boy, as the pair scuttled away behind their own dust cloud?

Apparently Christian was ready to trust his own hand and eye.

"Give me that rifle," he said. "I'll do the job myself! Here!"

And there he stood, settling the rifle to his shoulder.

It seemed to Bill Naylor that he could see again the puckered face of the boy, frightened, fighting against fear and conquering it. He leaped up and knocked the rifle of Chirstian off the bead that had just been drawn.

"Don't chance it chief!" he exclaimed.

Christian whirled on him with the face of an ugly devil. He drove the butt of the gun against Naylor's head hard enough to fling him flat on his back. As he lay there, gradually pushing himself on his elbows, he heard the hammer of the rifle fall with a dull click. The gun had misfired, and far away the boy had passed behind the screen of a grove of trees.

CHAPTER XXI

Suspect

SOME one shouted that they must run the boy down. Christian hurried off to the side with another rifle, hoping to get another shot at the target, but the youngster did not appear again except for an instant as he rounded the shoulder of a hill half a mile away and was quickly out of view again.

Five men were on fast horses, only waiting the signal before they spurred away, but Christian said to them calmly:

"No use, boys. That boy weighs only a feather, and by the way the legs of that mustang twinkled, it's a little speedster. We've simply had a break of bad luck."

He turned toward Bill Naylor, who was gradually picking himself up from the ground.

"At least," said Christian, "bad luck is what we can call it for the time being."

His voice was perfectly quiet. His eyes were still and calm, also. But it was the brightness of a steel point that was glittering deep in them. There was not the least alteration of feature in the man, and yet Naylor knew that he was ready to drink hot blood.

"Seemed to me a risky thing, chief," said Naylor, holding his injured head. "I didn't see how even you could shoot at that pair without chancing hitting the kid."

"And suppose I had?" demanded Christian. "Suppose that I *had* hit the boy? What of it?"

Naylor said nothing. He had a perfectly definite impression that if he had uttered a word, no matter what, he would be murdered on the spot.

Christian said to him softly: "I've owed you several things. They're wiped out. We start level again, Naylor, unless you *did* get the word to Jim Silver last night."

He meant it. There was no doubt about that. If ever Christian had even a fair suspicion that Naylor had carried that warning to Jim Silver, there would be death, there would be a death more hideous than fire for the traitor.

Christian had turned from Naylor to the others, and he was saying:

"Boys, this is a bit of hard luck. But the game isn't finished. It's several miles from here to Elsinore. Ordinarily it would require a good bit of time, in a town like that, to get together a posse to come out after a crowd like ours. But these are not ordinary times. You can see, now, why I wanted to get rid of Jim Silver last night.

"He's back there in Elsinore, unless some kind devil

129

moved him to leave the place to-day. He's there in Elsinore, and the instant the news is brought in by that lad riding horseback, Jim Silver will know what's up. He'll have a crowd together inside of three minutes, and be pelting out here to get at us. There's only one thing in our favor, and that is that the train is due in ten minutes. If everything works smoothly, we'll be able to put the deal through before any interference comes this way from Elsinore and Jim Silver. Get back to your places and wait!"

They went back solemnly.

Pokey paused beside Naylor and looked him curiously in the eye.

"How'd you like it?" asked Pokey, and then, grinning, he sauntered on his way.

The whole band would turn against Naylor now. He had been too high in the favor of the chief before. He was too low in that favor now.

He sat down, muttering savagely to himself. He had been right, he knew, in disturbing the aim of the chief. He was glad that he had done it. Other people would be glad to know that he had been man enough to interfere even with terrible Barry Christian for such a purpose as that. Sally Townsend would be glad. Jim Silver would be glad, too.

As for the personal indignity, he hardly felt it, for he would never have dreamed of comparing himself with the bright glory of Barry Christian. But it seemed to Bill Naylor, as the minutes passed, that he was being carried on wings far away, and far away from the whole purpose of his old life, in which Christian had been a hero.

Some one was calling in a rather hushed voice: "The train's already ten minutes overdue, chief. If we wanta have space between us and Jim Silver, hadn't we better start making tracks now?"

Barry Christian stood up. He said:

"Boys, every one of you can do as he pleases. I don't want any one of you to stay here with me unless he

130

wants to—except Bill Naylor. The rest of you are perfectly free to run and save your scalps. If I'm left alone, I'm going ahead with this job, anyway, and if Jim Silver comes up in the middle of it, we'll simply try to show him that bullets can cut through his flesh as easily as they cut through ours!"

It was a good talk, delivered with the right sort of a ring in the last words. It was greeted with a faint cheer, and Naylor knew that not a man of the lot would actually withdraw. That was what proper leadership meant. He wondered what this same Barry Christian could accomplish if he had behind him an army of honest men, and himself could fight with an honest purpose?

There was something else for Naylor to think of, and that was the entire attitude of Barry Christian toward him. He was now suspect, which meant that to-morrow he might be dead.

He was still in the midst of these broodings when some one called:

"I hear it! I hear it comin' out of the ground!"

There was something ghostly in that announcement —all the bright heat of the sun could not remove the suggestion of a spirit transpiring from the solid earth. But then, with his own ears, Naylor heard the faint and distant humming of the heavy iron wheels on the rails.

"All right, boys," Christian said. "The thing is going through like a song. Remember, I'm going to crack that safe if I have to do it with my hands and my teeth. There's several hundred thousand dollars waiting for us. Everybody steady. Everybody cool. Think of the scare we'll be throwing into the poor devils in that train—and don't shoot at a man until you see him flash a gun! A few rounds in the air as we close in, that's all!"

Bill Naylor repeated his own part to himself. He was to get close to the cab of the locomotive as soon as possible and cover the engineer and fireman. Cassidy, on the other side of the track, would be busy with the same task. They were the foremost of the gang stationed to get at the head of the train. Though it seemed to Naylor, as he looked down the rails, that sanded tracks and heavy brakes would surely bring the train to a halt much more quickly than had been anticipated after the engine rounded the curve of the valley.

In that case, might not the engineer be able to throw the gears into reverse and back the huge weight of the train away from the danger spot? Once under way, it would be an easy matter for the armed men in the train to keep off three times as many horsemen as Christian could offer for the battle.

These were the doubts that rose in the mind of Naylor as the sound of humming increased along the rails and then the distinct noise of the engine was heard. But he had prefigured a sort of heavy thundering of steam exhaust and laboring metal, such as a big train makes when it pulls up under the hollow of a vault of a station house, and he was amazed and taken by surprise when the engine suddenly poked its nose around the bend and came grandly on.

It looked as tall as a tree, and from its stubby smokestack a column of smoke shot swiftly back, expanding, spreading out in a flowing cloud like a half-divided head of hair. Then the engineer seemed to see the obstacle that crossed the tracks. There was a wild hooting of the whistle, and the brakes screamed, and the wheels skidded with a terrible vibration on the tracks.

CHAPTER XXII

The Train Robbery

BILL NAYLOR looked right and left toward the hooded figures. They were not simply equipped with face masks. Barry Christian always insisted that his men wear hoods that completely covered the head. Otherwise telltale features such as hair and ears could usually be glimpsed and serve as bases of identification in case of arrest. Naylor himself was wearing such a mask. He wished now that he had made the eye holes even smaller. It was better to endanger his own accuracy of vision a little rather than to expose too much of his face.

In the meantime, the train rumbled nearer. It came to a shuddering halt with the engine exactly in front of Naylor, and he sprang suddenly to his feet with a yell and fired a rifle bullet into the sky. That was the arranged signal. He felt, as he saw the train halt right in front of him, that the robbery could not fail to go through perfectly. The skill with which Barry Christian had estimated the distance the engine must cover before the brakes brought it to a halt offered an assurance that all the rest of the scheme would go through smoothly.

All down the line of the train, in answer to his signal shot, he heard an outbreak of shooting and yelling. Frightened faces looked out the windows of the coaches. But just before him he had his main concern. There was a gray-headed, red-faced hulk of an engineer in the cab of the locomotive. He had leaned from view and reappeared again with a big revolver in his hand. Bill

Naylor, his bead already drawn, merely snipped the cap off the engineer's head.

"Drop that gun, you fool, or I'll brain you with the next shot!" he shouted.

The engineer, his hair tousled and on end, looked woefully down at the big Colt which was in his hand. At last he threw it out on the ground with a curse. Across the cab, Naylor could see the fireman with his arms stiffly extended above his head. That meant that Cassidy was doing his share of the work.

In the distance he heard a voice shouting: "Open the door or we'll blow the car off the track, and you with it!"

That would be the mail coach which the robbers were threatening. But his own task was merely to see that the engineer was made helpless, together with the fireman, and that the fire box of the engine was thoroughly flooded. He told Cassidy to take the fireman down on his side of the engine. Then, climbing into the cab, he put his rifle aside and laid the muzzle of a revolver against the chest of the old engineer. He sat in the cab with his head fallen, his greasy hands weak, idle, palms up in his lap.

At Naylor's command to flood the fire box, he returned with a vacant stare:

"I dropped my gun like a dirty yellow coward—but I'll not lift a finger to kill this engine."

Naylor felt a sudden touch of pity.

"You're not disgraced," he said. "You got no chance. That's all. Buck up and do what I tell you!"

But there was no use arguing. The engineer seemed actually to prefer shooting to obeying orders from robbers. Cassidy had to get the fireman to do the job, and as the flood of cold water hit the raging furnace of the firebox, it exploded into steam that rushed out in enormous clouds with whistlings and rumblings. The cloud enveloped the whole locomotive and the head of the train, while voices of alarm yelled to cut down the fog.

In the meantime, Cassidy and Naylor tied the engineer and fireman back to back and elbow to elbow, which is about the best way of quickly making two men harmless, because every struggle of the one is sure to hurt the other.

There was plenty of action for Naylor to see as he walked back down the length of the train.

The passengers were making enough noise to furnish out a whole battle scene, but what mattered was the attack on the mail coach. The guards had failed to open the doors, and as Naylor left the engine and started back, a petard which Christian had affixed to the door of the mail coach exploded and smashed the lock. The door itself was instantly opened, and from within two repeating rifles opened a rapid fire.

The very first shot caught Dick Penny, of the Christian gang, full in the chest. He spread out his arms and walked with short steps across the tracks as though he were a performer on a tight rope striving to get his balance. He sat down against the fence and pulled off his hood in order to get more air. His whole chest was covered with red that began to leap down into his lap.

Naylor, taking shelter close to the side of the train, saw that picture. Then he was aware of a figure climbing apelike up the end of the mail coach and running along the top of it.

That was Barry Christian. No hood could conceal the dimensions of his big shoulders. And what other man, unless it were Jim Silver, could combine such massive weight and strength with such catlike agility?

When he was just over the open door, Christian got a toe hold on a ventilator in the roof and drooped his body over the edge of the car. In that way his head and shoulders swung down suddenly over the open door.

It was a maneuver so daring that it seemed suicidal, but in each of Christian's hands there was a revolver. He fired three or four times as fast as he could. Then he pulled himself back to the roof of the car.

The rifle fire inside the car had stopped.

"Go get 'em boys! They're done for!" shouted Christian.

135

The last of his words were blurred by a horrible screaming that began inside the mail coach. It made Naylor want to close his eyes and stop his ears, like a child or a foolish woman. He had never heard in his life a sound that was quite so frightful.

Big Duff Gregor, now that the rifle fire was silenced, was the first into the mail coach, with two others behind him. They pulled out two badly wounded men. They were carried over to the fence beside the railroad where Dick Penny was already sitting, and a yell from Christian told Naylor to guard them. It struck Naylor like a bullet—to hear his own name shouted out like that in the hearing of so many witnesses. Why should he be identified out of the entire crowd?

However, he had his hands full of work.

One of the guards had been shot through the body. He looked greenish white, he was so sick from his wound. He never made a sound of pain, but he kept saying in a weak voice:

"Quit the yelling, Charlie! Quit the noise!"

Charlie was not fatally hurt, in spite of his screeching. He had a clean bullet wound in his left leg, but what tortured him was the smashing of his right hand. A slug of lead from Christian's gun had drilled right through the center of the hand, tearing to pieces all the delicate nerves of the palm. He kept holding the hand by the wrist. He would be silent for a few seconds, bending his body forward and back like a pendulum, and then the scream of agony would jerk his head back and distort his mouth.

Every time he yelled, Naylor felt the sound go through him like a sword—a red, flaming sword that filled his brain with smoke.

He fell to work as fast as he could to bandage up the wounds. Cassidy was there, too, not being definitely assigned to any other task. He took charge of Dick Penny. Out of the corner of his eye, Naylor was aware that the passengers were filing out of the train and lining up in a long, straight row beside the coaches.

It was a long train, and it was crowded. Three women had fainted. They were carried out by other passengers and laid in the shadow beside the train. Up forward, the steam was still gushing with a fainter hissing from the flooded fire box, and now and then wisp of the thin mist were blown back across the passengers. Duff Gregor was starting down the line of them, searching them thoroughly, and dropping everything he got—jewelry, watches, wallets—into a canvas sack.

In the meantime, of course, Barry Christian and his chosen assistants were working on the blowing of the safe in the mail coach. They must be working with set teeth and hasty fingers, struggling against time, and in their minds, constantly, the image of Jim Silver rushing across the hills on Parade, with his followers streaming out behind him.

But all of these things were in the background of Naylor's mind. What immediately focused his attention was the screeching of the man named Charlie, and the doings of the other two wounded men. The guard who had been shot through the body was so sick and weak that he had slumped down on his back. He shook his head when Naylor offered him a drink of whisky from a flask.

"Just stop Charlie from screaming, will you?" he pleaded.

"I'm tryin' to stop, Mike," gasped Charlie. "But I can't! I'm tryin' to——"

And again the horrible outcry tore his throat.

Over on the left, Cassidy stopped trying to work for the comfort of Dick Penny. He wanted to make Penny lie down, but Dick refused. He was only nineteen, a stringy, blond-headed, cheerful youth with a string of killings chalked up to his credit.

"I'll take mine sitting up," he said. "If you don't stop that blankety fool from yelling, I'll shoot the other hand off him. Gimme a drink, Bill."

Naylor handed him the flask. Penny could not manage it with one shaking hand, but he succeeded by using two in getting the bottle to his lips. He took a long swig.

"I wish I could get the whisky into me as fast as the blood is running out," said Dick Penny. "That'd be a fair exchange. Here's to you, Bill!"

He drank again. He began to laugh, but the pain which the laughter caused to him cut it short.

Then he said—and Naylor never forgot it—"How dark it is, and not a star!"

Cassidy had the soul of a rattlesnake, but this speech had moved him.

"You're goin' to be all right, kid," he said.

"Shut up, you fool," answered Dick Penny. "I know what kind of a darkness this is. I know what kind of a night it is that's shutting in on me. I ain't going to wake up from this sleep. Gimme another flask, somebody. There ain't anything in this bottle."

There was no other flask at hand. Naylor said to Charlie:

"Can you shut up for a minute? My partner here is passing out."

Charlie bit a scream in two and swallowed the inside half of it. The other wounded guard turned his head toward Dick Penny and watched with eyes that were suddenly bright.

Penny said, "Help me stand up, boys."

"Sit still, Dick. You ain't fit to stand up."

Penny cursed him with a burst of language, saying: "I ain't goin' to sit down. I'm goin' to stand up to it."

Naylor understood what was in his mind, and, grabbing him under the armpits, lifted him to his feet. He supported him. Penny's head flopped over to the side, and his sombrero fell off.

"Put my hat back on my head," said Penny.

Cassidy lifted the hat, actually dusted it, and then settled it carefully on the head of Penny. The blood was running rapidly down to the feet of Penny. He was a crimson figure.

"All right, Bill. Let go of me," directed Penny.

"Are you sure, Dick?" asked Naylor.

"Shut up, and do what I tell you to do, will you?" commanded Penny.

Naylor gingerly released his grasp. He expected Dick Penny to fall flat, but instead, Penny supported himself on sagging knees. He turned, staggering, toward the others.

"Look!" he said.

"I'm watching," said Naylor.

"You tell the others," said Dick Penny in a voice suddenly clear and loud, "that I took it standing. I didn't lie down to it, and I didn't sit down to it. I took it—standing!"

His voice held out right to the end of his words. Then he crumpled up.

Naylor grabbed for him, but the loose weight slid through his hands to the ground. He looked down and saw the half-open eyes of Penny, and a small, sneering smile on his lips.

He knew very well before he fumbled at the heart of Dick that he was dead.

Then he heard Mike, the guard, saying: "That was pretty good. That's the best I ever seen. That's nerve, is what it is."

Right on the heels of that came an explosion that made the mail coach rock, and a thin cloud of smoke puffed far out through the open doors.

139

CHAPTER XXIII

Riders from Town

CHRISTIAN was first through the doors of the mail coach again. His shout of triumph told Naylor everything that he needed to know. The safe had been cracked, and the rest of this business would soon be finished. But where was Jim Silver, and where were the men from Elsinore that the boy on the fast-galloping mustang must have roused long before this?

A horse was brought up to the side of the mail coach, and Christian and the other men inside the car began to hand out hastily filled small saddlebags which were rapidly tied onto the horse. The thing was ended in another minute. Christian jumped down and whistled three quick notes.

"Fall in! Fall in!" he called in his great voice.

If any of the passengers on the train had ever heard that voice before, how could they fail to recognize now the powerful, ringing notes of it?

There was a quick scampering. The passengers had been disarmed, of course, as they were searched, and there was little danger that they would open fire as the retreat began. All that happened as the outlaws rushed to their horses was that one of the women who had fainted sat up suddenly and broke into hysterical laughter. She was a big, fat woman, and she laughed so convulsively that her hat jerked off her head and her gray hair tumbled down over her shoulders. She kept on laughing, on a higher and a higher note. It was strange the distance at which that laughter still followed in the

140

ears of Naylor as he rode away with the rest of the gang.

It seemed to him a mockery of all that had been accomplished on this day.

Cassidy rode up beside him as he took off his hood. "They say there's more than the three hundred and fifty thousand. They say there's nearly half a million taken out of that safe!" said Cassidy. "It takes Barry Christian to plan a scoop and then make it."

Naylor heard the words, but the meaning did not register deeply in his mind. Nothing mattered very much to him except the picture of how Dick Penny had stood up to die. As for the money—well, money cannot teach a man how to die. It can't do much of anything for you. You can't eat gold. And as for enough clothes to stand up in and enough food to eat—well, any fool can get those things by working honestly with the hands.

Who need be afraid of work?

He kept thinking along those lines while he jogged his horse in the middle of the crowd.

"That fellow Mike," he said to Cassidy. "Think that he'll pull through?"

"I saw where the bullet socked him and where it came out. He's got a good chance," said Cassidy. "But what d'you care?"

"Well," said Naylor, "it just makes the difference between robbery and murder."

Cassidy stared at him.

"Are you weakening, Naylor?" he demanded harshly.

And suddenly he reined his horse away, as though he were too disgusted by the last remark to remain any longer in the company of the man who had made it.

They got out of the narrows of the valley and onto the rolling uplands beyond, with Barry Christian keeping the pace down to a steady trot. That pace would conserve the strength of the horses, and if a posse from Elsinore came at them, probably the men from the latter town would have ridden most of the wind out of their mounts before they came in sight. But what man, other than Barry Christian, would have had the nerve to keep to such a moderate gait instead of trying to speed away for shelter among the higher mountains?

Gravely and bitterly, Naylor admired the outlaw chief. And yet, even at this minute he hardly regretted that he was no longer one of Christian's tried and chosen few. He was back in the ruck, part of the rank and the file. He noticed, too, that Christian was not leading the horse that carried the treasure. Instead, the horse was being conducted by Duff Gregor, whose fine thoroughbred chestnut stallion, stained to resemble Parade, was dancing lightly over the ground.

They had gone so far from the scene of the robbery that it seemed to Naylor that the late affair was sifting down into his past, joining many old memories that were dim under the sea of time, when the voice of Cassidy yelled:

"They're coming! They're coming!"

He looked back, and through a cleft among the hills behind them Naylor saw a slowly rising cloud of dust. It streamed toward them. He could make out little figures that moved under the cloud of the dust.

There was an irregular checking and spurring of horses. Then the calm voice of Barry Christian called:

"All right, boys. This is what we expected. Every man steady, now. Get the horses into a lope and keep 'em there. I've got a half-million-dollar flag here, and I know I can trust you fellows to rally around it!"

Of course, that was true, and a very neat effect it made to see that horse which was burdened with nothing but the stolen treasure. Not a man was apt to fall away from the party before receiving his split of the loot.

They went off steadily enough, riding at the lope, the pace for which was set by Barry Christian. And, looking over his little band, Naylor remembered the evening not so many weeks before when he had smoked at the side of the Kendal Falls and had seen the body of

142

the drowning man swept headlong down the current. Then, by a gesture—rather, by the lack of a gesture— he could have prevented all of this. He could have let Barry Christian pass on to the doom he deserved. Instead, he had chosen to pull him back to safety, and so he had managed to undo how much of the good work of Jim Silver?

Conscience was not a keenly developed portion of the soul of Naylor, but something like it was being tormented now!

They kept on at the steady pace until they had risen well up on a higher tide of hills, and at that point Christian fell to the rear and ordered the others to continue steadily toward a point which he had marked out.

Then, taking up his post on the brow of the hill, Christian drew out a strong field glass and peered down at the lower ground over which the pursuit was sweeping. He remained for some time conducting his examination. In the meantime, as the fleeing riders climbed a still higher slope, Bill Naylor in turn twisted in the saddle, let his horse go a little distance at a walk, and peered with straining eyes at the lower plain.

The pursuers were far closer than they had been a little time before. They came on with a determined rush, and the size of the dust cloud seemed to indicate more than a hundred riders in the lot. That, however, was too large a guess, for as a gust of wind cleared the dust suddenly away, Naylor was able to estimate the situation at a glance.

There were fully fifty men riding to the front, more or less stretched out in a loose formation, according to the strength of their mustangs and their skill as riders. And, a little distance behind them, held in a close herd by several other riders, appeared a sweeping mass of perhaps threescore unsaddled horses.

Fear that had remained far back in the mind of Naylor until this moment, now suddenly leaped up right into his throat. With so many remounts, the men of Elsinore would surely have an excellent chance of riding down Christian's party. But, more than all else, to make the picture significant, there was sight of a man in the lead of all the rest, and the horse he rode on flashed like gold, even from the distance.

That was Jim Silver and Parade.

CHAPTER XXIV

Christian's Scheme

THE news which Barry Christian now carried up to the party, riding at a sweeping gallop, was already clear in the mind of Naylor, of course; but he wondered vaguely how the chief would communicate the bad tidings. Surely he would hardly dare to reveal the worst! But perhaps others, though they had not lingered behind like Naylor, might have seen the dust cloud lift.

At any rate, Christian, rising in his stirrups, shouted in a loud voice:

"Boys, Jim Silver and the Elsinore men are coming like wild Indians. They've got a whole drove of remounts with them, and they're going to run us down before the day's over."

He made a pause. Cassidy's snarling, barking voice called in answer:

"Split up the loot now and we'll all scatter!"

"Is there time to split up the loot?" demanded Christian. "Before we can sort that stuff Silver will be right on top of us. No, we've got to stick together. But I have an idea of a way to beat them still. Boys, we're going to head straight for Benton Corner!"

A shout of dismay and confused doubt answered this suggestion. But Christian went on:

144

"We've got the double of Jim Silver with us, and I know how we can use him. Friends, we'll go right into Benton Corner. On the way there, some of you sling an arm; some more of you get a bandage tied around your heads or legs. A few little spots of blood here and there will make it look as though we've been under fire sure enough. When we get into Benton Corner, Duff Gregor will shout out the news that Barry Christian is on the loose again, that he's raised a mob of fifty men, that he's heading straight for Benton Corner to shoot up the town, that he—Jim Silver—has tried to stop the rush and failed. He'll call for volunteers to go out and meet the men of Barry Christian.

"You understand? When the Benton Corner men hear that, they'll turn out, every soul of 'em, and while they ride back to smash the charge, the rest of us will slip away through the town, scattering right and left through the alleys and the lanes. We'll come out and rejoin on the farther side. Understand? And we'll leave the Benton Corner and the Elsinore men fighting like fools too far away from one another to make out the truth!"

It took a moment for the details of the plan to penetrate the minds of the outlaws. But when they realized, they raised for big Barry Christian only such a shout as despairing men can lift in honor of a chief who promises them their lives. They yelled. They stood up in their stirrups and swung their hats and cheered for Christian. And Duff Gregor galloped to the side of Barry Christian to receive the final instructions before the town of Benton Corner was reached.

It was a neat idea. It might very well work, unless there happened to be in Benton Corner men cool-headed enough to realize that Jim Silver—the real Jim Silver—was hardly the sort of fellow to retire at a gallop even in the face of danger of odds of four to one. Unless, also, there happened to be some one who knew intimately the face of Silver and the figure of the great Parade.

What a man was Barry Christian! No wonder that
145

the cream of the criminal brains of the West was eager to follow him wherever he might lead.

Then the thought of Naylor turned back to Jim Silver, riding with the men of Elsinore on behalf of the law. No doubt, close to him rode that slender panther of a man with the pale, bright eyes—Taxi. Those two alone might be strong enough to wreck all the forces of the great Christian. It seemed to Naylor a battle of supermen—and he was a useless force in the encounter.

They turned straight for the town of Benton Corner, and as they journeyed through the heightening hills, the dust cloud behind them crept closer and closer, now working up to them with a continual sweep which made it clear that Silver had mounted his men on the reserve horses, and that he had determined to have the hounds of the law on the traces of the desperadoes before long.

No doubt he had not even stopped to make inquiries at the train that had been robbed. In the distance he would be able to see the big train standing with no smoke yet rising out of the stack. That sight, near the spot which the boy must have reported, would have been enough to tell him what had happened—that, and the gradually diminishing head of a cloud of dust in the distance.

Benton Corner, that must be the salvation of the fugitives, now heaved into view, perched between two hills, with the upper mountains just beyond it, and with the eternal smoke of the great smelter rising above it in an entangling mist that seemed to keep the little town drab and gray even in the midst of this beautiful weather.

There was not much wastage of paint in Benton Corner. It was a workaday town, and the houses in it were the color of decaying, weather-rotted canvas. There were no trees rising over it. There was no sense of pleasure in life when it was viewed from a distance or close up. Into Benton Corner swept the rout of the Barry Christian gang.

The orders of Barry Christian himself had been put

into execution faithfully. There appeared three men with bloodstained bandages around their heads. Two others carried one arm in a sling. There was a leg bandage here and there—and always there was the spot of red blood.

A desperate appearance they presented as they galloped through the streets of the town.

Here Duff Gregor became suddenly the most important man of the lot. Barry Christian himself had a face almost covered by a great bandage that must suggest itself to some observers as being useful as a mask as well as a protection to an injury. And Duff Gregor, his part already well rehearsed, and his brain crammed with words learned from Barry Christian, galloped before the rest on that beautiful, commanding figure of the chestnut thoroughbred.

As he went he shouted loudly, drawing rein a little. Behind him came the bandaged, the sweating, dusty, grim band of fighters. And as he galloped, Duff Gregor was yelling.

"Barry Christian's come back to life! Barry Christian's on the go! He's back there with fifty desperadoes. Any fighting men in Benton Corner?"

Any fighting men in Benton Corner? Well, there were no other sort of men in the town, truth to tell. And they swarmed out from lodging houses, from saloons. They broke up the groups which they had formed at corners, idling, and they bolted for their horses. At every hitch rack stood tough mustangs, saddled and ready for action, and here and there in groups there were men tougher than the horseflesh they used. No man had to wait to get a gun. Weapons they carried under their coats or belted around their thighs, or else they had long-barreled repeating Winchesters thrust deep in the saddle holsters, waiting to be used.

Fighting men in Benton Corner? Why, the whole town rose up, shouting, and started a dust cloud rolling out toward the direction from which, according to Duff Gregor, the danger was sweeping toward the town.

What amazed Bill Naylor most of all was the devotion, the veritable joy of these men when they saw that made-up figure of Duff Gregor and cheered him under the name of Jim Silver.

That name was always, on all sides, beating through the air. "Silver!" "Silver!" "Parade!" "Jim Silver and Parade!" they yelled as Duff Gregor went by, never pausing long, and always shouting out his warning, and then dashing on before men had a full chance to center their eyes on him and criticize the truth of his appearance.

There was one great fault in the performance—Jim Silver, the real Jim Silver, would hardly come plunging into a town like this, shouting for help, but—well, what Westerner would be critical? The very name of Jim Silver was enough to put all criticism to sleep and leave, in the place of logical, reasoning brains, a frenzy of hope and courage and excitement.

Benton Corner sent out its men like a cloud of dust that winged off through the hills to find the bloodthirsty followers of "Barry Christian." And this false "Jim Silver," who was expected, of course, to turn behind the recruits and rally the forces of battle outside the town?

Well, that "Jim Silver," like the rest of the rascals who were with him, turned aside and sneaked down a side street after he had seen the rush of fighting men start for the scene of conflict. Down alleys and by lanes they rode. One small boy, as Naylor would never forget, ran out in front yard and yelled at him: "That's the wrong way! Jim Silver wants you back there! Back there!"

Naylor jogged his mustang on its way. And the boy ran out into the street behind him and screamed:

"Coward! Coward! Jim Silver wants you!"

What a man, thought Naylor, if he could put himself inside the minds of the boys of the community in this fashion!

But, after all, the youngster was right. That was

148

where all the honest and brave men belonged—back there, helping Jim Silver, among the hills.

Before Naylor came out on the farther side of Benton Corner he could hear the distant sound of rifle fire from the other side of the town. And he knew that they were at it. Honest men against honest men, shooting to kill, one side led by the invincible name of the great Jim Silver, and the other side led by Jim Silver himself!

What a thing it was to divide a man against himself and use his famous reputation to destroy him, as Barry Christian was using Jim Silver now!

In the meantime, the other members of the gang had come sifting through the town. They were gathering together again, in a string, as a wedge of ducks might be scattered by gunfire when they fly near the ground, but reform again in the sky, after a short distance. That was what had happened with the Christian outfit. Here they were again, at the mouth of a great ravine that cleaved through the mountains as though they had been ripped apart by a gigantic plow.

Every man of them had reassembled, except Dick Penny. He was gone forever to another sort of a meeting, and another sort of a meeting place; there were only twelve men, counting the great Christian himself, who entered the mouth of the ravine in a group—and one of them was leading the treasure horse!

It seemed incredible! They could not, ordinarily, have dared to come close to any town, fugitives as they were from justice. Only the brilliance of Barry Christian had enabled them not only to pass through the town in safety, but to make of the law-abiding men in Benton Corner a filter through which what dangers could flow toward them?

Far in the distance they heard the faint clattering of the rifle fire only gradually dying away!

It seemed to Naylor that the back of Barry Christian was a little straighter. Certainly he had proved as almost never before in his famous career what a right he had to be called a lord of men. All his men were laugh-

149

ing, and they were slapping on the back Duff Gregor, who had just saved their hides! He was laughing most of all, that Judas whose life had been spared by the mercy of the great, the true, the honest Jim Silver!

Near the mouth of the ravine, the party halted at a place where a fresh spring bubbled sparkling out of the ground and ran brimful a little crater of rock. The big mountains shoved their naked heads up into the sky upon all sides. There was not a tree in sight.

There they halted, loosened the cinches of the horses, let them dip in their heads almost to the eyes to drink of the pure water. They sloshed water over the legs of the animals. At the direction of Barry Christian they led them up and down and gave them a good breathing spell.

For Christian pointed out that they had only won one lap in the race—unless by the fortune of war a bullet had happened to tag Jim Silver.

He even kept one man posted at the mouth of the ravine to give warning in case any one of a suspicious nature should advance toward them during the rest period.

It was a very jovial pause. Every one of the men, with a single exception, seemed as light hearted as a cricket. For when had criminals before this day ever managed to make the men of the law fight one another for the sake of a band of plunderers?

The one exception was Bill Naylor, and as he stood with gloomy head, watching his gray mustang, he suddenly looked up and felt the cold, bright eyes of Barry Christian fixed upon him.

With a shudder, Naylor looked away, for he felt that the cold, bright thrust of that glance had found his heart and opened up all the dark secrets of it.

Then, amazing them all, the guard who had been posted at the mouth of the ravine ran back, shouting:

"Jim Silver! Jim Silver! He's coming, with half a dozen men behind him! Jim Silver!"

The name rang magically on the ear of Naylor. He looked at Christian, and for the first time he saw the face of the great outlaw blanch. Was it surprise or fear that had unnerved him?

CHAPTER XXV

The Trap

THERE was reason enough for Christian to be dismayed. What had happened? How had Silver managed to disentangle himself from the fight on the farther side of the town? How had he managed to sift through so quickly with a chosen band of the pursuers?

Then Christian came to himself and said calmly: "Boys, this puts the crown on everything. Scatter back on both sides. Get those horses out of sight among the rocks. You hear me? Get everything out of sight, and see that your rifles are loaded. Every man pick his target —but leave Jim Silver to me! I'll take care of him!"

He made a brief pause as he shot home the last order with a stern glance of his eye.

Then he added: "Now move!"

They moved on the jump. One glance around the place showed them that it was a perfect trap. Even if Jim Silver had led his original two or threescore men from Elsinore straight into the mouth of this funnel among the mountains, it seemed likely that the dozen sure rifles could curl them up in a red ruin and thrust them back.

Naylor, automatically taking shelter behind a great black boulder, found none other than Duff Gregor beside him. And with Duff Gregor was the horse that carried the treasure.

They were well up the side of the mountain; they had a good slant to look beyond the mouth of the ravine out onto the lower ground from which Silver must approach. And Naylor heard Gregor snarling:

"There's one thing that makes me sour, and that's Christian reserving Silver to himself. I'd like to sink some lead of my own into Jim Silver. I could ride the real Parade as well as the next man."

"Christian's a funny guy," said Naylor slowly. "Maybe he thought that you'd feel sort of kindly about Silver since he saved your life for you and turned you loose from the men of Crow's Nest."

Gregor growled: "That what you say? I'm goin' to have words with you after this little job's over and we've mopped up Silver and his gang of fools."

Suddenly curses streamed out of the lips of Naylor. He said savagely: "It ain't *words* that you're goin' to have with me, you swine!"

Gregor, unexpectedly, said nothing at all.

And then, through the gap in the mouth of the valley, Naylor had a sudden glimpse of the advancing party.

There were not six men. There were only five men— and a bare-legged youngster who rode without a saddle on a tireless little mustang. The very boy who had discovered them and had carried the alarm!

He was one. There were four others, of whom one, from his size and the way he kept close to Jim Silver, was probably that other famous man of battle, Taxi. But most of all, foremost in the lot, magnificent on his great, shining stallion, came Jim Silver himself.

Something stood up in the heart of poor Bill Naylor and called that hero his master. And something told him that it was better to die a thousand times on the side of such a warrior than to live forever surrounded by Christian and his crew.

Suddenly Naylor rose.

152

"Hey! Don't show yourself, you fool!" cried Gregor. "They're almost where they can see——"

Naylor laid the barrel of a Colt along the head of Gregor, and with satisfaction listened to the ring of the hollow steel. He watched Gregor drop, and then he deliberately flung himself into the saddle of the horse that carried the treasure and started as wild, as desperate, as hopeless a charge as ever a man attempted in this world. For he made the mustang bolt, under frenzied spurring, toward the mouth of the ravine, straight out to give warning to Jim Silver of the deadly trap which he was approaching.

His horse had not taken three strides before a voice was shouting:

"Hey, you crazy fool!"

That was Cassidy. No other voice had the bull-terrier, whining note of battle as did the voice of Cassidy.

Then the stentorian shout of Barry Christian bellowed through the air: "Shoot the traitor! Shoot him!"

And the rifle fire began.

Down the steepness of the slope the flying mustang ran as a torrent of water runs, plunging from side to side, angling away from projecting rocks, dodging like a snipe in flight from the hunter, and not a single bullet struck lucky Bill Naylor.

Well, bullets didn't matter. If he could let some blood, it would carry away in its flowing some of the sins of his life, and help to wash his soul clean.

The horse hit the level of the valley floor beneath. The gunfire increased. The thunder of it rang all about him, until it seemed from the echoing that a thousand guns were working.

Then a blow struck him on the back between the shoulders, not like a bullet, but like a club. The weight of the shock knocked him forward over the pommel of the saddle. His whole back was benumbed. Afterward there was a shooting thrust of pain right up into his

153

head; and after that the pain spread inward toward his heart.

"They've shot me through the heart," his numb lips said to him. "Why don't I die? Heaven won't let me die till I've warned Jim Silver!"

Aye, but Jim Silver was already warned, surely, by the clamor of guns inside the death trap that he had so nearly entered. Then why could not Bill Naylor stop the mustang and slide down from the saddle and stretch himself on the ground?

To lie there, stretched on the ground, for a moment's respite from the agony that was wearing away the strength of his soul!

Then he understood why he must keep on riding. It was because he was carrying with him, back to the hands of the law, the treasure for which one man had died already.

He was going to die, too, he told himself. He wanted only to die like Dick Penny. That was the way to meet the end!

But the best he could do was to scurry away like a frightened rabbit with a bullet through his back!

Well, a man like Jim Silver would understand.

The mustang staggered suddenly and almost flung him from the saddle. The horse had been hit. And as Naylor righted himself in the saddle with dreadful labor there was another shock and numbing blow as a rifle bullet struck him at the hip from behind and tore through his flesh, and glanced around the thigh bone and came out above the knee.

"What kind of luck is this?" said Bill Naylor. "They're going to shoot me out of the saddle—but I got the hoss pretty near to the mouth of the ravine already."

A wave of darkness washed across his brain.

Another shock, another club stroke. He didn't know where that blow had fallen, but now there was warm blood flowing down over his face.

"I can't feel nothing no more," said Bill Naylor "except my heart—except my heart."

That agony devoured all that was inside him, all the heart, all the spirit, all the courage.

Then, like the opening of a door, he was through the mouth of the valley, and on either side of him the bright-green of the outer plain extended. He saw a group of riders halted. He saw the brilliant sheen of Parade. That was, in fact, all that he could see very clearly.

Jim Silver would have to be in the saddle on that horse.

So he made for Silver.

He saw the wink of light along leveled gun barrels, and he heard voices shouting to him to halt, and then the cry of Silver bidding the others to hold their hands. Then, suddenly, he was drawing rein, or trying to, beside Silver.

But he could not draw rein slowly enough. The wounded mustang came to a pitching halt that slewed Bill Naylor out of the saddle and rolled him on the grass. Every time he rolled he left a spot of blood. He rolled over and over twenty times, and when he looked to the side he could see the crimson trail that he had made on the grass.

Better on grass than on rocks. Far better on grass than on rocks!

The blue sky was revolving around him like a spinning wheel. He was being lifted up into the blue. He was somewhere high up, among the bright drifting of the clouds.

Then a voice boomed in his ears. He looked with a vast effort.

"Silver," he said. "Is that you?"

He could see nothing, only the whirl of the blue; but the voice of Jim Silver, wonderfully deep and gentle, was saying:

"I'm Jim Silver, partner."

A faint smile pulled at the numb lips of Naylor. Partner? Well, it was just as well that Silver did not

155

know the darkness of his past! And for five minutes to be esteemed noble by such a man, was not that enough?

"Silver," he said, "they're in there, waiting, I seen you coming, and couldn't stand it. I got on the hoss that carried the loot from the train. It's all there. Watch yourself. They're all in there. Barry Christian and ten more!"

"Barry Christian!" cried Silver. "Barry Christian?"

"Yes," murmured Naylor.

Then, distantly, he heard the voice of Silver saying: "Taxi, stay here with him. Watch him as if he were yourself. Keep the kid with you. I'll scout on ahead."

CHAPTER XXVI

The Way to Go

IT WAS the sort of a thing that every one knows how to appreciate, for it was the sort of thing that every man of us hopes may be possible in himself—a change forever from the bad to the good.

They found out all about Bill Naylor while he lay flat on his back in the hotel room in the little, grimy town of Benton Corner. The newspapers found out; they lived on the trail until they had located his associates of older days—most of them in prison, and most of them willing to talk. They found the marshals and sheriffs who had arrested him in the past and the posses that had assisted on occasion. Some of these informant grinned and shook their heads, but most of them had pleasant things to say. A crook? Sure, Bill Naylor had been a crook, but he had always been the sort of stuf

156

that can turn straight when the right time comes for turning.

Honest men, reading their newspapers of a morning, shook their heads and smiled, also. They were pleased. We have all done shady things, cruel things, evil things; and we all hope that we will never do them again. The story of Bill Naylor helped every man to believe in himself a little more, to have faith in that higher self which obscurely struggles with the baser.

But Bill Naylor, as he lay in his bed in the hotel room in Benton Corner, knew very little about all of this for many days.

The first thing that he was aware of when he opened his eyes and discovered with bewilderment that a weak pulse of life was still throbbing in him, was the almost handsome face of Taxi. The pale, bright, dangerous eyes were fixed steadily upon him.

"By thunder, Taxi," said Naylor unevenly, "how come you're here?"

"I'm the wake," said Taxi with a faint smile. "I'm waiting—and it seems as though you're going to wake up and live out the rest of your days. You've got to. If you don't, Silver will hound me around the world."

Naylor looked at the ceiling. He wanted to shake his head, but there was hardly enough strength for even that gesture.

"That's funny," he said. "Jim Silver, he wants me to pull through?"

"Jim Silver's not a hound," said Taxi. "He wants you to live through. Because—I'll tell you a queer thing—Jim Silver is sort of fond of a man who's saved his life twice in a row!"

Naylor considered this thing curiously with a detached mind.

"Jim Silver's still on the out trail, I suppose?" he asked.

"And he'll never leave it," said Taxi. "Not till he's run Barry Christian to the ground. If Barry Christian were the devil and could take a thousand forms, I think

157

Silver would find 'em one by one and strangle them all. It's the end for Christian."

Taxi sat close beside the bed. His eyes were set back in deep, dark hollows. His face was drawn.

"You go to sleep again," he said. "Because now I'm going to have a chance to do a little snoozing on my own account."

And Naylor, dreamily smiling, went back to sleep.

It was a long time after that when he wakened again. Then he heard a girl's voice saying:

"I wouldn't bother him none. I just wanted to look at him."

That was the voice of Sally Townsend, and the voice of her father muttered:

"Don't you be a fool, Sally. He's gone and got himself famous now. He wouldn't be wanting to see you."

"Sally!" said Bill Naylor.

There was a whispering of clothes. She stood above him.

She looked better in overalls than in store clothes, with a foolish hat perched high on her head, and her hair pulled back so tight that her eyebrows were raised a little.

She looked like a small girl dressed as a grown-up. He had to squint and glance back into his memory before he could recall her to his mind as she was before— as she really was.

She was frightened. Her eyes were too big for the pupils. They showed a lot of white all around. And she had gloves on her strong brown hands. Suddenly he wanted to get her away from the sight of every one. Out on the range—that was where she belonged.

"Hey, Bill!" she said in a husky whisper.

"Hey, Sally!" said he.

"Shall I get out of here?" asked the soft voice of Taxi.

"Wait a minute," said Naylor. "Meet Sally Townsend How I wish that Jim Silver was here to meet her, too."

"Jim would like to be here, I know," said Taxi.

158

"This is Taxi," said Naylor. "And this is Sally Townsend, who's promised that she'll marry me."

"Jiminy!" said the girl. "Are you Taxi? Are you *the* Taxi?"

Taxi took her hand. He said that he was happy to meet her. He only wished that Jim Silver were there, too, because he said that Jim Silver thought a great deal of Bill Naylor and would want nothing so much as to see the girl he was going to marry. He said that they would all have to be good friends, because they all belonged to Silver's side of everything. It was quite a speech, quite a pretty speech. Taxi was capable of them, now and again.

Then he got out of the room, but big Townsend came and stood at the foot of the bed. He had shaved off his ragged beard, and his face looked boyish and rather pale, except for the dark tan around the eyes. And he had on a high stiff white collar that choked him. The necktie had worked down and showed the brass sheen of the collar button.

"Well, Townsend, I'm lucky I'm not up," said Bill Naylor.

"Why?" asked Townsend, gaping a little.

"Well," said Naylor, "if I was up, you'd lick me because I'm trying to get Sally. I'm a lot safer in bed."

Townsend grinned. Sally sat down on the edge of the bed and took Naylor's hand.

"You've talked enough," she said. "Dad, go on away."

Townsend went away.

"When you get better, we'll talk a lot about things to come and the way we're going," she concluded firmly.

"There's only one way to go," said Naylor.

"What way is that?" asked the girl.

"Straight," said Bill Naylor.

159